8/26/20

CORNFLOWERS AND CORPSES

CORPSES

PORT DANBY COZY MYSTERY #13

LONDON LOVETT

CHAPTER 1

*E*lsie pulled the hot loaf of zucchini bread out of the oven. My nose wiggled into action. "I smell cinnamon."

Lola scoffed as she picked up her coffee. "You don't need a super nose for that. Even I can smell the cinnamon. Since our little get together is after the lunch hour and before the dinner hour, is it called a linner? Or is it a dunch?"

"How about just a munch fest?" Elsie placed the steaming brown sugar loaf on a plate in the center of the table. We'd decided to have a girls' late Sunday afternoon get together, complete with all the goodies we could muster (most of which had come straight from Elsie's oven).

"My vote is for munch fest." I reached for the first hot slice of sweet bread. It was dotted with chunks of walnuts and thin wisps of zucchini. "You are truly a miracle worker, Elsie. Who else can make a vegetable into such a delectable, decadent treat?"

"Any other person who has baked zucchini bread," Elsie quipped as she sat down to join us. She reached for some of the plump red strawberries Lola had brought. "Although mine is probably better than most." She arched a judgmental brow toward Lola, who was deeply focused on slathering an obscene amount of fresh whipped butter on her slice of zucchini bread. "How on earth do you stay so skinny?" Elsie asked.

Lola shrugged and shoved the richly topped bread into her mouth.

"It's because she never stops moving," I said. "And it's aggravating as heck."

Elsie turned the same arched brow my direction. "Says the woman who consumes bakery goods like other people drink water. And you're still the same size you were when you danced into Port Danby a few years ago with your hopelessly positive attitude and your flower arranging notebooks."

I grabbed a thick, green slice of honeydew melon. "Hopelessly positive? I'm not hopelessly positive."

"Yes you are," my two friends said in perfect unison.

"Really?" I smiled. "Then I'll take that as a compliment."

"See," Lola said. "Hopelessly positive." A burst of wind sprayed Elsie's kitchen window with drops of rain. Lola groaned. "Why is it raining? It's June. I want perpetually sunny weather from this point forward. No clouds or rain or anything that frizzes my hair for the next three months."

I wiped a touch of butter on my zucchini bread. Lola was a terrible influence. (Not that I needed influence.) "Rain will make the rest of summer, including the sweltering month of August, even more beautiful."

"Yes, all right, *Pollyanna*," Lola quipped. "Now you're trying too hard. But I know a subject that even you can't put a positive spin on." She rested back with a pleased smile. "Does your new flower arranger start tomorrow? What will that be, number four or number five?"

I sighed deeply. "Six if you count the guy who showed up an

hour late on the first day and then asked which flowers were chrysanthemums before proceeding to engage in a lengthy text conversation with his gaming buddy. He was there for such a short amount of time, I can't even remember his name. But I do remember that he'd had something with garlic for breakfast because he smelled as if he had spent the night in a vat of garlic infused olive oil."

Elsie pressed a napkin to her mouth to stifle a laugh.

I pretended to be offended with a chin lift and a straightening of my posture."I'm glad you find my plight so entertaining."

A dry laugh burst from Elsie's mouth. "Excuse me but you told me you were going to write a book about all the baking assistants I've blown through in the past two years. I'd say that falls under the category of entertainment."

"Yes but you have not had as many assistant disasters as I've had in just two months time," I said. "May I remind you about Norton and his planetary mission."

Lola laughed. "Did I hear this story? I don't remember the planetary mission."

I turned to her. "That's because while *I* listen to all your problems thoughtfully and with all the great care of a true friend, you wave off my grievances as not even worthy of a furrowed brow."

"Not true. I was highly concerned about your wonderful assistant, Ryder, leaving you in the middle of bridal season." Lola picked up another berry.

"I'm pretty sure your concern was more about you missing your boyfriend than me having to run around with my hair on fire all while putting together bridal bouquets."

"What happened with the planetary mission?" Lola took a bite of the berry.

"It was all going well. Norton, a thirty something college graduate in—" I cleared my throat. "In philosophy," I continued.

"That should have been your first clue," Elsie quipped over the rim of her coffee cup.

"For two days, Norton had helped me put together six bridal bouquets and fifteen centerpieces for a large wedding. He was talented and seemed to know his way around a flower arrangement. Not like Ryder, of course but I was pleased. I thought this guy would work out and my troubles were over. The bouquets were delivered. Norton was leaving for the weekend, and I said 'see ya Monday'. He glanced back and said 'oh, I have to return to my home planet next week. My planetary mission here on Earth is over.'"

Lola sat back so hard with laughter the chair tipped back on two legs. "Can't believe you didn't tell me this. Did you ask him which planet?" she said after catching her breath.

"First of all, I did tell you, but I'll refer you to my previously mentioned comment on you never listening to my lamentable tales. And no, I didn't ask because, frankly, I was stunned speechless. I swear even Kingston's eyes were bulging in disbelief, as if he'd understood the entire statement."

Lola crumpled back into another bout of laughter. "I've had some silly shop assistants, but that one takes the prize. Poor guy. Do you think he was serious, or maybe he just didn't like working for you?"

I exchanged annoyed glances with Elsie. "Thank you for that, but I'm fairly certain he was serious."

Elsie picked at her slice of zucchini bread. "Maybe he was telling the truth," she said offhandedly.

Lola laughed again, then paused to see if Elsie would join her. She was wearing a perfectly serious expression as she scowled Lola's direction.

"I'm just saying that none of us know for certain. There could be aliens walking amongst us here on earth," Elsie said curtly.

They were the most unexpected words to ever come out of my highly pragmatic, logical friend.

"Elsie," I started cautiously. "Is there something you're not telling us?"

Lola sat forward clumsily and the table wobbled. "Oh my gosh, Elsie, are you an alien? Is that why you have superior baking talents? Did you come from a place where trees are made from pastry dough and rivers flow with whipped cream?"

Elsie casually picked up a grape from the fruit plate and threw it across the table at Lola. "If I did come from a place with whipped cream rivers, do you really think I would have decided to live here instead? I confess, I occasionally watch those programs that theorize about ancient aliens and beings from outer space. There, now you know the real me."

I reached over and patted her arm. "I think it's good that you let your mind loose occasionally, Elsie. And you're right. Maybe Norton was actually telling the truth."

"Oh no," Elsie said. "That guy was off his rocker."

We sat in silence for a second, then burst into peals of laughter. It was our usual girls' outing, good food and lots of fun. I wouldn't know what to do without my two good buddies, both delightful and entirely unique in their own ways. (Although, I was still having to process Elsie's earlier confession about her interest in aliens.)

The laughter died down, and each of us refilled our coffee cups. It was an unusually cold and rainy day for June. Hot coffee and the yummy cozy atmosphere in Elsie's kitchen were just what we needed to make the event perfect.

"At least Amelia has worked out. She is great with the customers. She even helps out with purchase orders." I put my cup down. "If only she knew how to arrange flowers. She tried a few times, but she's like a—what's the saying—like a bull in a china shop. She breaks every flower."

Lola rested back on the chair. "So, what you're saying is that it takes not one but two people to replace the wonderful, magnificent Ryder Kirkland." She smiled and gazed up into the air as if she'd been pulled into a daydream.

"You're trying to imagine what it would be like if there were two Ryders, aren't you?" I asked.

Lola shrugged. "You know me too well, but just think of the possibilities."

"Right now, I definitely wish that were the case. Then one Ryder could be having the time of his life studying rare plants in the Amazon, and the other could be helping me at the flower shop. Unfortunately, there is only one Ryder, which means Barbara Malcom, the *highly qualified* flower arranger, better show up on time tomorrow with a good attitude and a healthy belief that she belongs here on this planet. I'm so desperate for help, I had to hire her over the phone. She seemed quite knowledgeable, and her resume was impressive."

"Well, I hope she works out," Elsie said. "By the way, are you going to check out the bird watcher's convention in Mayfield? They've ordered eight dozen of my shortbread cookies in the shape of doves."

"I'd heard there was a bird event in Mayfield," I said. "But I hadn't really considered going."

"I just thought, you know, since you are sort of closely associated with a bird that you might be interested." Elsie got up to carry the empty plates to the sink.

"Closely associated with a bird?" I laughed lightly. "That's a weird way to put it, but I don't know if being the personal servant for a demanding crow puts me in the category of bird enthusiast."

"The flyer I saw said they would be selling all kinds of bird toys and treats and other goodies a bird owner might need," Elsie said as she turned back to the table. "Might be some fun stuff there."

"You just want someone to go with you when you have to deliver your cookies," I said.

"Possibly," Elsie admitted.

"I'll take you up on it if you go late in the afternoon when the flower shop hits its lull in customers. Amelia is getting comfortable enough with the flow of the shop to work the customer counter without me for a few hours. It'll be good practice for her. And who knows, maybe I'll find something to make the world's most spoiled crow even more spoiled."

CHAPTER 2

The June rainstorm had cleared out by Sunday night leaving behind a stellar Monday morning that was scented with the crisp fragrance of trees and flowers. My newest assistant, Amelia Stratton, was standing in front of the flower shop cradling a cup of Les's coffee between her hands as if it was winter. She brought the cup to her mouth and pursed her lips to blow on the hot beverage. She was just attempting a cautious sip as I reached the storefront.

Amelia was in her late twenties with sparkling brown eyes and a gracious smile that helped her easily win over customers. She moved quickly and efficiently. She'd been working in hospitality, including as a cruise ship activity director, for the past six years, and that experience made her an expert in customer service. She'd quickly learned how to write up big orders and answer all manner of questions that pertained to flowers. Unfortunately, she just couldn't arrange them.

Amelia flashed her warm smile as she held up the coffee. "Last Friday I took a sip too fast and couldn't taste anything for the entire day, so I'm taking my time." She glanced around. "Where's King—" she started but didn't need to finish.

Kingston came flapping out of a nearby tree. After his clumsy descent, he landed gracefully on the arm of the bench outside the shop.

"There you are, King," Amelia said cheerily. It was the same tone she used for everything. No matter who she was talking to or what she was doing she always spoke as if she was meeting her best friend or greeting guests at a restaurant. She was particularly fond of my bird, although the feeling wasn't necessarily mutual. Amelia tended to move just a little too fast for Kingston's liking.

I unlocked the door and we walked inside. The shop was filled with the light, sweet scent of the five dozen electric blue cornflowers that were waiting, in all their blueness, to be tucked between white roses for wedding bouquets. They were a vibrant, hearty flower with a faint scent, unless you were sporting a nose like mine. Then five dozen in a small space could produce quite the perfume.

"What time is the new flower arranger coming?" Amelia asked as she headed straight to the office to put away her purse.

I followed her. "She should be here soon." The shop bell rang as we put away our things. "That might be her now."

"I hope she's from this planet," Amelia whispered. She had witnessed, firsthand, the parade of unsuccessful flower artists that had come and gone in the past two months.

"Me too," I whispered back.

I walked to the front of the shop. A forty something woman, small and petite with thick glasses was talking softly to Kingston as he slid back and forth along his perch trying to decide if the stranger was friend or foe. The woman was wearing a bright pink shirt with the words Bird Nerd printed across the chest. She didn't match the image I'd formed of my new assistant.

"Barbara?" I asked hesitantly.

The woman spun around. "No, my name is Nora."

"I'm sorry. I thought you might be my new floral assistant. How can I help you?"

"I'm not here to buy flowers." Nora swung her purse around to the front and reached into it. She pulled out a piece of bright yellow paper. "I was hoping I could hang this flyer in your shop window. The West Coast Bird Watching Society is having a convention in the next town, and we're hoping to attract a large crowd. I saw this lovely crow in the window and had to come right in to see him. Is he a pet?" Her lip was turned up, and there was a noticeable amount of judgment in her tone. I'd come across more than one person who seemed to think I was wrong for keeping a wild animal as a pet, so I already had a well-scripted answer.

"More accurately, I am *his* human. I rescued Kingston and brought him back to health, but when it was time for him to head back into nature, he decided he preferred my waffles and hard-boiled eggs."

Obviously, considering herself a bird expert (as noted by her t-shirt) she wasn't buying my answer as easily as other opinionated people before her. She turned back to Kingston. "Wouldn't you rather be soaring through the blue sky, hanging out with other crows?" she asked and even paused for Kingston to respond.

"I assure you he does plenty of soaring in blue skies, and he prefers the human race to his own." I added in a nice, curt tone to assure her the debate was over. "I would love to hang your flyer in the window," I added with a polite smile, even though I wasn't feeling all that polite.

She looked momentarily puzzled. "Oh yes, the flyer." She handed it to me. "Thank you so much and be sure to attend. There are many beautiful perches and bird toys for purchase. For parrots and other pet birds, of course, but I'm sure your crow would find them entertaining. They are one of the smartest birds," she said confidently as if telling me something new.

"Trust me, once you've lived with a crow, you find that fact out pretty fast." I glanced at the flyer. According to the long list, a visitor could buy everything one might need to keep a pet bird or go on a successful bird watching adventure. Entry included free entrance to all of the various lectures and slideshows from club members.

"This is quite an event," I said. "I guess I'll see you there." I'd already made plans to go with Elsie, but I decided to let Nora think she'd talked me into attending.

"Great," she said with a nod. "Well, I'm off to visit that lovely lighthouse at the end of the road. I'm hoping to spot some Shearwaters gliding out over the waves. They usually don't show up until fall, but I'm hoping to get lucky."

"There are an abundance of birds out on the beach. I'm sure you'll spot many species," I said.

"I'm mostly interested in spotting rare birds. We get points and prizes for capturing images of rarely seen species. What is the best route to the lighthouse?"

"There is only one. Take Harbor Lane to Pickford Way. That will take you directly to the lighthouse."

The front door opened as Nora turned around to say her goodbyes to Kingston. A woman in her mid to late thirties walked in wearing a blouse with a bright floral print and white jeans. Her brown hair was brushed up into a tight bun at the back of her head, a hairstyle that was more suited to someone much older. Her brows were penciled in with uncommon precision and at such an arch that they gave her a somewhat permanently surprised look. Her footsteps were sharp and efficient, reminding me of Elsie's stride, as she walked across the floor with her hand out in front of her.

"You must be Lacey Pinkerton. I'm Barbara Malcom." She took hold of my hand before I could answer.

"Yes, hello. I am Lacey." I waved briefly at Nora as she walked

11

out of the shop, then turned my attention back to Barbara. "You're certainly dressed for arranging flowers." I smiled at the blouse that was covered with yellow peonies and pink carnations.

She glanced down at her attire. "Yes, I believe in thoroughly immersing myself in my work."

Amelia cleared her throat to remind me she had yet to meet the new assistant.

"Oh, yes, Barbara, this is Amelia, my other assistant. She handles the customer service and phones."

Barbara and Amelia shook hands and nodded politely. I was getting a good feeling. Maybe I'd finally found my team. I'd already decided that even with Ryder's return, the business was doing well enough to add on additional employees. As it was, I'd had to turn down a few large orders because we were too booked. I was slightly giddy at the notion that the shop was doing so well that I needed more help. And now, with any luck, I'd found that help. Of course, Barbara still needed to prove herself as a flower arranger, but after seeing her resume, I was certain I wouldn't be disappointed.

Barbara and Amelia ended their little impromptu chat, then Barbara turned to me. "Point me in the direction of the flowers and we can get started."

CHAPTER 3

*P*ink's Flowers was running like a well-oiled machine. Amelia covered the flow of morning customers, while Barbara and I created splendid cornflower bouquets. Barbara was fast and accurate with the flowers. Every bloom in its place and jutting at just the right height and angle. She might have been just a little too exact. Both Ryder and I leaned more on creativity and spontaneity while creating bouquets, but I was pleased with her efficiency. The only flaw I could find was that she insisted on tidying up each one of my bouquets too. I tried not to be insulted and thanked her for correcting my imperfections. (Even if I didn't truly find them to be imperfections.)

After a whirlwind morning, the shop had finally hit a lull. Kingston was feeling ignored after the chaos. He let out a sharp caw to remind me he was sitting on his perch, neglected and hungry. The unexpected sound startled Barbara, causing her to drop a spool of pale blue ribbon. The spool rolled along the floor, leaving a long tail behind it. She looked miffed about the whole thing, but I couldn't tell if she was angry at herself for dropping the spool or at the crow for startling her. I soon discovered it was the latter.

Barbara had been focused and mildly pleasant for the entire morning but now her face stiffened as she stared across the shop at Kingston. "Does that bird stay in the shop at all times?" she said it with a slight grimace of disgust. "Surely, he'd be happier outside with the other birds."

It seemed I was about to once again enter into a debate about my bird's happiness. Her sudden change in demeanor and attitude put a kink in what I'd otherwise deemed a successful morning.

"Kingston loves being in the shop," Amelia piped up. "And most customers adore him." She was right to add in the qualifier *most*. While he had a slew of fans, Kingston was not universally adored. Mayor Price, for example, was terrified of him. Unfortunately, Barbara seized on that one word.

"Most." She laughed airily. "Even if most customers find the bird an interesting fixture in the shop, you don't want to risk scaring off the people who don't enjoying having a big black raven scowling at them while they pick out flowers."

Amelia opened her mouth to respond, but I smiled and winked her direction to let her know *I* would do the responding this time. Barbara had done a great job. She was exactly who I needed for the busy bridal season, so I didn't want to upset her. I also needed to set her straight.

"Kingston is part of my family," I started and continued right past her amused grin. "He is a crow and not a raven. He is not a fixture. He is a member of this flower shop and people enjoy seeing him. I think we can put an end to this conversation. I've got a list of single arrangements to create, two birthdays and three anniversaries. Would you like to start on those while I do some paperwork?" I knew my safest bet was to pull Barbara's attention away from Kingston and back onto flowers. She would get used to him soon enough and possibly even discover why so many people adored him. Hopefully.

Barbara wiped her hands on her work apron. "Yes, I'm happy to help with the single arrangements. Just give me the list, and I'll get started right away."

I was relieved that the crow topic had been dropped. I headed into the office to grab the list of orders.

Amelia's cheery tone rolled down the hallway. "Good morning, Detective Briggs." She giggled. "Or I guess I should say good after-noon since it's nearly lunchtime."

I headed back out to the front of the shop. Amelia was intro-ducing Briggs to Barbara. Barbara seemed suddenly much less stri-dent and more frilly, almost flirty.

"Nice to meet you, Detective Briggs," Barbara said with an overly gracious smile. She took a second to tuck the one thin strand of hair that had come loose from her bun behind her ear. She smiled again.

Briggs seemed relieved to see me."Lacey," he said abruptly. "I just stopped by to—" He paused when he realized Barbara and Amelia were still quite engaged in his arrival.

I motioned discretely with my head for him to follow me into the office where we could speak without an audience.

"Nice to meet you." Briggs nodded politely to Barbara and Amelia before hurrying after me down the hallway.

"I wasn't expecting you, but you sure sent a flutter of interest through my staff," I said quietly as we walked into my office.

Briggs wore a grin as he shut the door. "Your staff?" he asked. "Sounds very official."

"That's right. Pink's Flowers has a staff just like any successful business," I said proudly.

Briggs rarely missed an opportunity for a kiss. I certainly didn't mind. He pulled me closer and pressed his mouth briefly over mine. "You've done a great job with this business. You should be very proud of yourself."

"Thank you. I am."

He lowered his arms. "How is the new assistant working out?" he asked.

His question gave me pause. I had to think about it. I kept my voice low. "Not entirely sure yet. I think it's too early to tell."

Briggs had left his suit coat back in the office. He always looked great in a dress shirt, especially when he had the sleeves rolled casually back, exposing his strong forearms. Today, with the summery weather, he had even loosened his tie. The casual detective look was really working for him. No wonder Barbara and Amelia were in such flirty moods.

"Was she clumsy with the flowers?" he asked. Briggs knew that Amelia had worked out great with everything except flower arranging. He was always tuned into my business, almost as much as I was tuned into his work when there was a good murder case on his plate.

"Actually, she's great with arrangements. Fast, efficient and knows exactly what she's doing." And all of it was true. I couldn't think of one deficiency in that department. Still, there was something that didn't sit right. Briggs always knew when I had something on my mind.

"But—" he started for me, knowing full well I'd fill in the blank.

"Well, it's silly really. I shouldn't even care because she'll be a big help to me."

"But—" he repeated and stretched the short word out to a long one.

"It's just that she kept putting finishing touches on *my* bouquets. Mostly, it was just a little adjustment here and there, but it felt a little insulting. Like I was an apprentice and the master was showing me how to do it right." I waved my hand. "I feel stupid even talking about it. It was no big deal. She has a keen eye for detail and obviously likes everything to be perfect."

"Is that really necessary for flower bouquets?" he asked. "It seems like flowers are in themselves less than perfect. Each one a little different?"

I smiled at him and reached up to straighten his collar. "Aren't you the philosophical nature lover today? I like this side of you. Although, if I'm being honest, I like all sides of you."

I laughed as he pulled me in for one more kiss.

"Can you overlook her quest for perfectionism?" he asked. "It's better than—let's just say, if she's from this planet, she's already a better candidate than some."

"You've got a good point," I agreed. We kept our voices low. "Also, there was a little tense moment about Kingston. She doesn't seem too keen on the idea of a crow hanging around the flower shop."

Briggs nodded. "I can see where he might take some getting used to, but after she has realized he's really more human than bird, she'll forget he's even there." He glanced at his watch. "I've got to get back to the office for a conference call with some of the higher ups. They are considering adding a second detective to the area."

My mouth dropped. "Wow, that's a big deal. So you might get a partner?" I shook my head. "Never mind, you already have one."

He laughed quietly. We had debated about my unofficial title many times. I considered myself a partner, but he insisted I was an assistant. I just let him go on thinking that.

Briggs took hold of my hand. "How about we meet at Franki's in an hour for lunch? Then we can talk freely and not at a weird, low whisper."

"As wonderful as that sounds, I've already got a date for lunch. I'm meeting Marty Tate. He said he found another picture of Jane Price." Marty, the wonderful, old character who had been in charge of the Pickford Lighthouse for decades, had a collection of very old photos that belonged to his mother. His mother had been friends with Jane Price, the mayor's great aunt. I was sure Jane Price had been having an affair with Bertram Hawksworth, a romance that might very well have cost the entire Hawksworth family their lives. Marty's photos were all part of my research into the century old murder.

"I see, so I've been replaced by someone older and wiser," Briggs said. There was a smidgen of genuine disappointment in his tone.

"You could join us," I suggested.

"No, that's all right. But save a spot on your calendar for your boyfriend in the near future." He opened the office door.

"I will pencil you in, sir."

CHAPTER 4

*M*arty Tate and I met in Franki's parking lot. He looked a bit more hunched over than the last time I saw him, but his eyes sparkled like a kid's. His feet scraped the asphalt as he shuffled toward me. "Well, if it isn't my favorite florist?" His voice was a little more wobbly too. No one seemed to know quite how old Marty was, but it seemed he had experienced a great deal of Port Danby history. It was always a treat to hear him tell a story from a previous era.

I took hold of his slightly shaky hands. "And if it isn't my favorite lighthouse keeper." People inside the diner were already hopping up and peering out the windows. Marty was somewhat of a celebrity about town and for good reason. He was amazing.

"We should probably go in before your fan club rushes out here to greet you in the parking lot," I quipped. "I'm already preparing to be utterly ignored by Franki as she fawns all over her favorite Port Danby customer."

Marty's chuckle was low and had a marvelous gritty quality that I loved. "I suppose we should make our appearance. I'm hungry too. I was out of my usual frozen waffles this morning, so I had to settle for a banana."

I looked at him sideways as we headed inside. "Frozen waffles? I had you pegged more as an eggs and toast kind of guy."

Marty smacked his lips. "I've been eating a waffle every morning for forty years. Maybe that's the secret to living a long, healthy life. Frozen waffles and maple syrup."

"Sounds right to me," I said.

A chorus of shouts met us as we stepped into the diner. "Marty! Hey, Marty. What pried you out of that great white tower?"

Franki came sashaying over with a smile that she saved especially for Marty. It was sort of a cross between a flirty school girl grin and a glowing look of admiration that I was sure women in the fifties sported whenever Cary Grant or Gary Cooper walked on screen.

I'd already discovered that I became invisible whenever I was with Marty, so I didn't feel too insulted when Franki smiled directly at him. "I've got your table all ready." She practically sang the words. Franki was generally a polite and well-rounded pro at customer service, but she turned into an entirely different person altogether when Marty walked into the diner. It was amusing to watch.

Marty, always the gentleman, waved me ahead. I followed Franki to Marty's usual table, a nice little double booth next to the front window. It had an unobstructed view of the lighthouse, in case he forgot what it looked like while eating a bowl of chili. Franki put the menus on the table and spun around with a smile that would win an Oscar. It slipped back to her regular smile when she realized it was only me behind her. Marty had, as usual, gotten tugged aside for a chat with three fishermen sitting two tables down.

"Oh, Lacey, hello," Franki said and then leaned to the side to make sure Marty hadn't slipped out unnoticed. "Hey, guys, let Marty sit. I'm sure he's hungry for lunch."

The fishermen ended their chat, and Marty shuffled toward the table. I slid onto the seat. With some effort and a few grunts, Marty settled himself into the seat across from me.

Franki started right in before Marty even had a chance to place the napkin on his lap. "I've got some excellent tuna salad, Marty. Or maybe you'd like one of those special cheeseburgers with the Thousand Island and pickles."

Marty smiled at me. The crinkles on the sides of his eyes proved he had lived with a lot of laughter. I hoped mine would look the same one day. (Hopefully, not any time soon.) "What are you having, Lacey?" he asked.

"Cheeseburger sounds good to me, and a glass of lemonade to wash it down." I handed Franki my menu.

"Make it two cheeseburgers and two lemonades," Marty said. "And a few extra fries," he winked up at Franki.

"You know I always give you extra," Franki gushed. She winked back and walked away.

I held my hands out pretending to measure the table. Marty's fuzzy gray brows did a little dance on his forehead.

"What are you doing?" he asked.

"The last time we were here, Franki brought you a platter of cornbread big enough for the entire diner. I was just wondering if this table will be big enough to hold the mountain of French fries."

Marty laughed. "That wit of yours. It's superb. Does James know how lucky he is?"

I tapped my chin. "I'm not sure. Maybe you should tell him next time you see him." I laughed to let him know I was only kidding. (Unless he felt inclined to do so.)

"You know something, I think I will," Marty said with a nod. He sat back and reached into the pocket on his sweater. It was a dark gray cardigan that had been worn so often there were dozens of tiny balls of wool all over it. He always wore a sweater, even in summer. I remembered my grandmother doing the same. His trembling fingers emerged with an old photograph. "I have no idea why my mother had this particular picture of Jane. It seemed to be addressed to someone Jane referred to as Teddy. My mother never had the nickname Teddy."

I nearly slipped off the seat at the mention of it. "Teddy," I said excitedly as I reached for the photo. Jane Price was standing in the town square wearing a flower adorned straw hat and a pale colored dress.

"It's a beautiful picture. She has a wise face, doesn't she?" Marty asked.

"She certainly does." I turned the picture over, finding it hard to contain my excitement. "To Teddy from Button," I read. "Oh, Marty, if it wouldn't make Franki jealous, I would lean over this table and kiss you."

His grin was ear to ear. "You make an old man blush, Lacey. Does this photo help? I hoped it would add to your collection of important evidence."

Our chat was temporarily halted by the arrival of our lemonades. Marty got an extra big glass with a slice of lemon resting prettily on the top. "Your burgers will be right up," Franki said, smiling only in Marty's direction. She hurried away.

I shook my head as I leaned forward. "I'll bet she ran out and freshly picked the lemons in your glass."

"Franki's a good girl. She's always very attentive," he said in the greatest under exaggeration of all time. He pushed his sweater sleeves back and rested his arms on the edge of the table. "So, let me guess—Bertram Hawksworth is Teddy."

"You are a great investigative partner." I took a sip of my lemonade and pursed my lips from the tartness. I picked up a package of sugar and set to work making it sweeter. "In my research, I've come across some love letters. They were hidden in a trunk in the gardener's shed, the makeshift Hawksworth museum. The trunk belonged to Bertram. The letters inside were written to Teddy and signed love Button. Naturally, I first considered that they were from Mrs. Hawkworth, his wife, Jill, but this photo confirms my suspicions. Jane was having an affair with Bertram, and she was carrying his baby when she was sent away from Port Danby."

Marty rubbed his chin. There were several thick, white hairs sticking out from it here and there. "Here's a theory, and remember this is my first try at detective work," he added. "What if Jill Hawksworth found out and went mad with rage and killed the family?"

I nodded. "Yes, she would have reason to be angry, but would she kill her own children? And if she had been the culprit, how did the gun end up in Bertram's hand?"

He sat back slightly deflated. "Of course, you're right. That's why I'll leave the detective work to the expert."

"Hey, that was a good theory. If I'm being honest, I never even considered the possibility that Jill Hawksworth had killed everyone in a fit of rage. She certainly had motive."

"Yes but the evidence doesn't line up with that theory. Somehow, the gun landed in Bertram's hand. She couldn't have killed herself and planted it there."

The smell of grilled onions and pickles wafted our way. Franki carried our plates to the table, including an extra plate that was filled with a tower of crisp golden fries. Franki set the fries down between us.

"Anything else?" Franki looked directly at Marty, so I could only assume she wasn't interested in my possible needs.

"No, this looks delicious, Franki." He grinned up at her, and she looked close to melting like butter.

"Just holler if you need something," she said as she walked away, adding in another wink for good measure.

Marty pushed the plate of fries closer to me. "The potatoes look good, crispy the way I like them. How about you?"

"Yep, crispy and golden." I plucked one off the top. "And, may I add, being your friend sure comes with a lot of perks, Marty Tate."

CHAPTER 5

'd only been gone from the shop for an hour, but apparently, it had been long enough for Barbara to take the initiative to move things around more to her liking. The rolling steel shelves that held a wide variety of vases and ceramic pots had been rearranged not by color, like I'd placed them in, but by size. The small display of decorative greeting cards had been physically picked up and moved to the other side of the center island. It was hard to know what the reasoning was behind the move, but it seemed Barbara knew. She stood proudly with her arms crossed and a confident grin plastered across her face as I took in the numerous changes she'd managed during my lunch break.

Amelia, on the other hand, crinkled small and quietly near the front window and next to a noticeably empty bird perch. She seemed to be waiting anxiously for my reaction. I was determined not to overreact. However, I was gritting my teeth hard enough to feel several grains of French fry salt lodged in a back molar.

"What do you think?" Barbara asked enthusiastically. "People have told me I'm a master at time and flow management. They were simple changes, really, but I think you'll find the work flow is much smoother."

I forced a smile. "Except that I was used to the other flow, the flow that's been in place for the last two years." It was like rearranging a kitchen and spending months going to the wrong drawer for the wooden spoon and the wrong cabinet for a glass.

Barbara waved off my comment. "You'll get used to it soon enough, then you'll see that my way is best."

I flicked a look Amelia's direction. Wide eyes stared out of a stone stiff face. Amelia shrugged so slightly, it would have been easy to miss. She didn't know what to think, apparently. But I did. My newest assistant was a control freak. Everything had to be done her way. I'd known more than one in my life, including my dear friend, Elsie. But it wasn't a bother when the controlling person wasn't trying to change me or my life or my store. This was a little harder to swallow. My mind swished quickly away from the notion of firing Barbara. I needed her skills. She knew she'd been hired on as a temporary position until my regular assistant returned, my wonderful, incredible and greatly missed regular assistant.

"We'll give your way a try," I said weakly. "Both of you can take your lunch now. I'll manage the shop alone." Again, my gaze floated Amelia's direction. She seemed to be signaling something with her eyes and the tilt of her head. She was pointing out the empty perch. She was worried about Kingston.

"When did Kingston go out?" I asked.

"Right after you left," Amelia said abruptly. The look of worry on her face intensified.

Barbara didn't notice. She hurried into the office to get her purse, then swept back out. "I'm off. I'll be back in exactly forty-five minutes." And I had no doubt it would be exactly forty-five.

The door shut behind Barbara and I turned to Amelia.

"What's wrong?" I asked Amelia.

She finally took a breath that she must have been holding forever. "First of all, I tried to tell her not to move things, but she insisted she knew better." There was an eye roll added to her comment.

I glanced toward the door to make sure Barbara hadn't returned for something. "It seems like there's more you want to tell me."

Amelia chewed on her bottom lip as she rubbed her hands together. That sinking feeling you get when you realize you've made a big mistake started to weigh down on me.

"It's just that—as soon as you left, Barbara insisted King should go outside. She said she wasn't comfortable with him lurking around while you were out. I told her he was perfectly harmless and friendly, but as I've already noted, she thinks she's always right. Well, King wasn't really in the mood to go out, so she sort of chased him out."

"Chased him out?" I asked. "You mean she ran after him?"

She nodded. "With a broom," she added grimly. "She didn't hit him, of course. She just used it to sort of shoo him out the door."

I sighed loudly. "Why would she do that? Poor King. He is probably sulking somewhere in a tree. I'm going to go out and look for him. Can you delay your lunch for fifteen minutes?"

Her mood brightened. "Of course. Yes, go find the poor guy. Then I can apologize to him. I should have wrenched that broom right from her hands. Are you going to fire Barbara?" she asked hesitantly.

"I don't know. I really need her help, but I'm definitely going to mention her treatment of Kingston." That statement rightly caused a fretful look on Amelia's face. "Don't worry. I won't even mention the broom. I'm just going to let her know that only I can let Kingston out of the shop. Hopefully, that will stop her from chasing him out. Now, I better head out and find him."

I had a few of his favorite places on my first spots to look list. If he was in a bad mood, chances were, he would head across the street and wait for Lola to let him into her shop. His big crush on my best friend made her store his favorite go to place. He also loved the table area outside of Elsie's bakery where he could indulge himself in a variety of pastry, muffin and scone crumbs. I turned that direction first and got lucky. My feathered friend was skittering beneath the tables, head down and beak fully ready to pluck up crumbs. He took a second to glance at me over his shiny black shoulder but then returned to his feast. It seemed he had weathered the incident without too many mental scars. I credited Elsie's cookie crumbs for saving the day.

A customer walked out and a swirl of lemon, butter and something more floral, lavender if I had to guess, floated out. (Only with my nose it wasn't really a guess.) It was lavender, an unusual scent that was usually more prevalent on my section of sidewalk than Elsie's. I left my crow to his crumb binge, the human equivalent, I supposed, of a pint of butter pecan ice cream after a breakup.

I opened the bakery door and was further pummeled with the lemon, lavender mixture. Elsie was placing a delicate, dove-shaped shortbread cookie into a cellophane bag. She glanced up only for a second and set to work tying the cookie bag up with a piece of lavender ribbon.

"Your timing is astounding. How did you know I have some broken shortbread cookies waiting to be tasted?" she asked.

"It's not all that astounding considering you always have something ready for a taste test when I walk in. Am I smelling lemon and lavender in addition to the butter and sugar?"

"You sure are." Elsie nodded and picked up another bird-shaped cookie. "I thought I'd liven things up a bit by adding lemon and lavender to my usual shortbread dough." She picked up a cookie that was shaped like a wing. "I think they turned out great."

I reached for the tender, crumbly cookie and ran it past my nose. "Fragrant." I took a bite and spoke past the cookie in my mouth. "Delicious," I mumbled and swallowed. "Tastes like summer. I think the bird people will love them."

Elsie laughed. "Bird people. Sounds like they should be walking around with wings tied to their backs and tail feathers sticking out of their pants." She motioned to her front window. "Speaking of birds—why does yours look so sullen? I walked out there to say hello and give him a peanut butter treat. He took it with hardly a glance my direction, as if he wasn't interested in any chat."

I looked back past the sumptuous chocolate cake in Elsie's front window and out to the sitting area. Kingston was squatting, looking lonely and sad, beneath one of the chairs. I turned back to Elsie.

"Apparently, my new assistant doesn't appreciate how extraordinary Kingston is. She shooed him out with a broom while I was at lunch."

Elsie nearly dropped the cookie she was holding. "Well, you'll have to fire her. How dare she do that to Kingston."

"I'm going to speak to her after she gets back from lunch. She also rearranged my shop while I was out."

She lowered the cellophane bag as her chin dropped open. "I wouldn't just fire her, I'd have her arrested."

I laughed. "Arrested? Might be a little extreme for someone who rearranged vases and ceramic pots."

Elsie shook her head. "If someone came in here and tried to rearrange my bakery, I would spit fire through this nose and steam would come out of my ears."

"Pretty visual you've laid out, but I know you're not over exaggerating. Fortunately, I'm not quite as set in my ways as you. Still, I'm going to talk to her. But I'm not ready to fire her. She is great with flower arranging. A little too picky and an annoying perfectionist but she's fast and efficient, just what I need right now. And after a string of terrible hires, I'm not that anxious to start the search again."

Elsie did a poor job of holding back a smile. "You mean it's hard to find a good assistant? I don't know what you're talking about. See, you just got remarkably lucky when Ryder walked into the flower shop."

"I see that more than ever now. I will no longer tease you, but I still say you are way pickier than me. Like you said, Barbara would have been long gone, forced out by flaming nostrils, apparently, and yet I intend to keep her on. But I will let her know that she can't treat Kingston badly. She needs to learn to ignore his presence and accept that he is an important part of the shop. I need to get back so Amelia can go to lunch. At least *she* has worked out. The customers love her." I turned to leave but stopped. "By the way, are we still heading over to the bird convention later? I think it might be interesting. Maybe they have a book on making your crow feel better if his self confidence has been shattered by a mean lady with a broom."

Elsie chuckled at that notion. "I'll be ready to go after I close up for the night. I need to deliver the cookies this evening."

"Great. I'll see you at closing then. Now, I'll head back to my shop and ignore all the annoying changes Barbara made. Hopefully, my bird will follow me, otherwise your bakery might have a new feathered fixture."

"Wait." Elsie walked over to the dog treat jar and pulled one out. She tossed it to me. "Lure him back with one of these."

"Thanks." I walked out. Kingston was still squatting and pouting underneath a chair. I held up the cookie, and he hopped up with a new look of enthusiasm. "Come on, King. Sometimes you just have to ignore humans. We tend to be an ignorant lot." I heard his tiny talons tap the cement sidewalk as he trotted behind me and the peanut butter treat. I was definitely not pleased with Barbara, but I just couldn't take the time to look for another assistant. I would have to swallow back the bitter taste and look past her many flaws. I couldn't let down my customers.

CHAPTER 6

$\mathcal{T}$he convention for bird enthusiasts was set up in the large Mayfield Auditorium that sat directly across from the town hall and public library. The parking lot was nearly filled to capacity as Elsie pulled in.

"Who knew a bird convention could attract so many visitors?" Elsie said.

"Guess there are more ornithology minded people than we realized." My own personal matters concerning birds, and one in particular, had been straightened out. Or, at least, I hoped that was the case. I'd made clear to Barbara that Kingston was to be treated as a member of the staff and that I was the only person who could let him outside. Her face was pinched and her mouth pursed throughout our one-sided chat, but in the end, she nodded and said she would not let him outside ever again. That was the end of the conversation. I considered letting her know that I didn't appreciate her moving my things around but then decided one lecture a day was enough. I could put up with a few changes in order to have good help. I foolishly told my latter decision to Elsie and had to be on the receiving end of a lecture about being far too soft with my employees. I told her if that's what it took to have a talented flower arranger, then I was willing to accept that I was a pushover.

The summer sun was still high enough in the sky to give a nice kiss of warmth to the early evening air. Elsie opened her trunk and handed me a box of cookies, then she grabbed the second box. "My contact here is Minnie Sherman. She's the club treasurer. She told me she'd be in the tiny office space near the stage and across from the bird toy vendor. Maybe a nice toy will cheer up that crow of yours," she suggested.

"He was cheery enough once Barbara left for the day. But boy did he keep his beady black eyes fixed on her for the entire afternoon. It probably wasn't the best move to ingratiate himself into her friend circle, but you know King. He holds a grudge."

"He's also a good judge of character. In his Edgar Allen Poe sort of way, he is cryptically trying to tell you something evil is afoot and its name is Barbara." We walked through a maze of parked cars and vans toward the entrance of the auditorium.

"Barbara is not evil. She is just controlling, and she doesn't care for crows. But until her bad traits outweigh the good, and by good, I mean her ability to create bouquets, she will remain at the shop."

Elsie shifted the box to one arm and opened the auditorium door. The roar of voices inside the cavernous room was nearly deafening. Elsie had to practically yell. "Boy, these bird people are boisterous. Let's head up toward the stage. That's where Minnie should be sitting. I texted her that I was on my way with the cookies."

I strolled along with the box but found it hard to focus on our mission of cookie delivery. There were so many interesting gadgets and trinkets related to the hobby and science of bird watching. We walked down an aisle that was lined with kiosks displaying a variety of tech devices to assist the avid bird enthusiast. One seller was demonstrating how to use a monocular device with a smart phone to get the perfect picture. It was small and sleek like a mini telescope and allowed the user to take a crystal clear photo of a bird a thousand feet away. There were stylish backpacks that allowed you to carry all your equipment easily and safely on your trek through the wilds. One kiosk was set up with a black canvas tent where attendees could walk inside and try out a night vision monocular for sighting those mysterious nocturnal flying creatures. There were spinning racks of outdoor gear and earthy colored hats to protect heads while not alarming the birds. One woman proudly displayed colorful all-weather personal field notebooks that allowed users to take them out in the middle of a rainstorm without the notebooks getting ruined.

As we neared the stage area, we passed the largest and most heavily trafficked kiosk. I stopped to gawk at the colorful display of bird toys. The owners of the company had brought two macaw parrots along to assist with demonstrations, which explained why it was the most popular booth.

It took Elsie a few of her purposeful, fast steps to notice that her cookie partner had stopped. She backed up. "We can look at this stuff on the way out. I need to catch Minnie in the office."

I nodded but couldn't pull my gaze from the incredible displays. Colorful geometric blocks of wood hung from a peg board overhead. Bells rang softly from the ends of brightly colored ropes. There were even yellow, blue and orange wheels that a bird could swing on or ride around like a Ferris wheel. "It's like an amusement park for birds. Look at that hammock. Couldn't you just see Kingston lounging in his little hammock in the shop window?"

"Just what he needs." Elsie tugged me along. "If I'd known it was going to be like taking a kid into a candy shop, I would have delivered these myself."

I trekked begrudgingly alongside her. "I had no idea how much fun this place would be. Maybe I should take up bird watching. There are so many neat tools and gadgets to go along with it."

The stage area was a large, glossy platform with a massive screen hanging at the back. Metal folding chairs were being placed in a semi-circle around the platform so that the screen could be seen from any angle. A projector and laptop were being set up for a presentation. A poster proclaimed that Nora Banks, the woman who had posted a flyer in my shop, would be presenting a slideshow that contained a *special surprise*.

"A special surprise," I muttered to my uninterested friend. "I'll bet it's a photo of a rare bird."

"You've already got a *rare bird*," Elsie quipped. A thick door was sitting slightly open just feet from the stage. Elsie tapped it with her knuckles, and a woman's voice invited us in.

The small utility room had been set up with a table and a computer. The entire room was heavy with the scent of the orange the woman sitting behind the table was eating. A pile of bright orange peels sat next to a metal box, the kind used to keep money.

The sixty-something woman had gray hair with pink streaks. Large gold hoop earrings dangled from her ears. Her bright orange lipstick matched the pile of orange peels. Her blue eyes landed on the boxes we were carrying. She took a deep whiff. "Wow, the orange I'm eating smells so strong that I can barely smell the cookies. You're Elsie, I presume. I'm Minnie Sherman, treasurer of the West Coast Bird Watching Society."

Elsie and I placed our boxes on the table as Minnie reached across to shake hands. I didn't have to smell my hand to know she'd left behind a citrusy scent.

Elsie opened a box and lifted out a cellophane bag. She had packed each individual cookie in its own treat bag and tied it off with a lavender ribbon to go with the taste of the cookie.

The room was lit only by the glow on the computer and the

light coming in from the crowded auditorium. Minnie picked a pair of glittery gold glasses up off her chest where they hung from an equally glittery chain. She put the glasses on and held up the cookie package, turning it back and forth to get a good look at the beautiful cookie inside.

A big smile erupted on her round face. "I love it. These will sell like crazy." She untied the ribbon and shrugged coyly. "I just *have* to give it a taste." She broke off the head of the dove cookie and pushed it past her bright orange lips. Her eyes closed as she chewed. "Hmm, that is delicious." Her eyes popped back open. "I'm getting a lightly floral taste. Is that lavender?"

Elsie nodded. "I thought it would go nicely with the lemon."

I pointed out the orange peels. "You must have good taste buds. It seems it would be hard to taste anything but orange. The whole room is filled with the scent of it."

Minnie put the rest of the cookie back in the bag. "It was a particularly fragrant orange. And you're right. I think I'll enjoy the rest of this cookie after the orange scent has disappeared." She placed both hands on the metal box and pulled it toward her, then fidgeted with the latch to open it. "I can pay you cash, if that's all right." Minnie said to Elsie.

"Sure, I never turn down good old fashioned cash."

Minnie counted out the money the club owed Elsie. She pushed up from behind the table. "Now, I think I'll take a break from this gloomy utility closet and do a little shopping. I spotted the cutest little, olive colored, insect proof hoodie that I need for my trip to South America." She waved her hands in front of her face as if scaring off a swarm of mosquitoes. "The insects are as thick as mud down there." She followed us out and shut the door behind her. "You two should stick around. There's going to be an exciting slideshow in a little while. One of our members captured a rare photo of a Northern Goshawk. We're all anxious to see it. Thanks again for bringing the cookies,

Elsie. They're perfect." With that, she hurried off toward the kiosks.

I turned to Elsie and gave her my best pleading look.

"Fine, we can stay for awhile, but I need some food. Let's go see if that baked potato stand has anything worth consuming. Although, I'm not getting my hopes up."

CHAPTER 7

*A*fter an, as expected, disappointing baked potato and an hour perusing the many kiosks geared toward owners of pet birds, I came to the conclusion that Kingston was nothing like a chirpy little parakeet or talking parrot. His beak wasn't really made for playing with toys or gnawing on colorful ropes. As for bells, he would probably enjoy one but as I considered a pretty brass bell tied on the end of a chain, I visualized myself being hailed to serve my bird, like a butler or downstairs maid.

"I can't believe there is this much bird merchandise," Elsie said. She rarely entered a kiosk and spent most of her time standing in the aisles avoiding people with parrots on shoulders and large cages being rolled through to waiting cars.

The bird watchers had their own little niche carved out near the stage area. It seemed activity on stage was ramping up and projector lights and microphones were being tested for the presentation. Like Elsie, I knew little about rare birds like Goshawks, but I was far more anxious to learn about them than my convention partner.

Minnie was sitting at a table. She had set Elsie's beautiful cookies out. A banner on the front of the table proudly boasted West Coast Bird Watching Society. Pamphlets filling event goers in on the benefits of being a club member were piled neatly around the array of cookies. A small placard mentioned that all proceeds from the cookie sales would go to the club for future events like the wonderful bird convention. It seemed as if the cookies weren't being plucked up too fast but then Minnie had put an exorbitant price of three dollars on each cookie.

"Three dollars," Elsie muttered as she spotted the table. "I sold them to her for a buck a piece. That's a big markup. No one is going to buy them at that price." Elsie's bottom lip pouted. She wasn't used to her baked goods sitting unwanted for long. That was when it occurred to me, there was nothing on the sign to let people know who baked the cookies. I was sure more than half the attendees were locals like Elsie and me.

"Actually, I think she will sell them for that price," I said. "She just needs to advertise them better." I headed across to the club table.

Minnie's hoop earrings dangled as she peered up at me. "Oh, it's you again." She glanced past me and spotted Elsie, who was wearing a less than happy face. Minnie leaned over the table to get closer. "I thought people would go crazy for the cookies. Do you think I should break a few up so they can taste samples?"

"I was just going to suggest that. Also, if you add a placard that states that the cookies are from the Sugar and Spice Bakery, I think you'll have these cookies *flying* out the door."

Minnie clapped once. "Great idea. I'll get right to it."

Elsie, not wanting to hear about her cookie failure, had wandered down to the next kiosk where a statuesque woman clad in stylish sports gear and black hiking boots was showing several people a large framed photo of a flock of geese in a perfect V flying through a dusky pink sky. Her entire kiosk was filled with framed photos, mostly of birds in nature but a few other critters made the cut too, like a black bear sitting against a tree in the midday sun and a herd of elk littered across a vast open field.

I joined Elsie to peruse the stunning nature photos. The sign above the entrance of the kiosk read Ivy Eagleton, Professional Nature Photographer. Beneath the bold blue letters, in parentheses, the words *and bird enthusiast* had been added in a much frillier font.

The woman, Ivy, I presumed, finished with her customers and turned to Elsie and me. "Thank you for checking out my photo collection. Let me know if there's anything you're interested in, and I can give you the backstory and location. I also have some books, one of which won an award from the World Ornithology Organization." Her photos were breathtaking, but unfortunately, so were the price tags. I would have to settle for looking at Kingston in his natural habitat, which included the back of my sofa and the cereal cupboard in the kitchen.

"You took all these pictures?" Elsie asked sounding rightly impressed. Some looked like difficult or even dangerous shots and all in seemingly exotic locations.

"Yes, I'm quite proud of my collection."

Ivy had a mouthful of very white, very straight teeth. She dressed and carried herself as if she'd come from money, money enough to let her travel the world and experience everything nature had to offer.

"They are wonderful," I added.

"Thank you. Like I said, if there's any particular photo you're interested in just let me know. By the way, I'll be closing up in about ten minutes. I'm anxious to attend a presentation from a good friend of mine, Nora Banks. You've probably already heard about her slideshow. Should be exciting. I, myself, have never been lucky enough to snap a photo of a Northern Goshawk. You should attend."

"I think we're planning on it," I said.

Elsie pulled her focus away from a framed photo of pink flamingos standing in a marsh. "We are?"

"Yes." I added a pleading smile. "In fact, we should head over to the stage and get some good seats. Your photos are lovely." Elsie followed me out of the kiosk.

"Why are we—" Elsie started, but her attention was drawn to the club table where Minnie was frantically trying to keep up with the cash being handed over and the cookies being swept up. Elsie's face lit up. "They're buying the cookies after all."

I took hold of her arm and led her toward the stage. "That's because Minnie added a sign that said Sugar and Spice Bakery."

"Yeah?" She pulled down on the hem of her shirt. "Guess people will pay for quality." The change in *cookie fortunes* improved Elsie's mood instantly. "I suppose we could stick around for a slideshow."

Nora had changed her t-shirt from Bird Nerd to one that just had silhouettes of various birds printed across the chest. She looked more than a little nervous as she stood behind the projector and picked up the microphone.

Her slightly shaky voice echoed through the building. "I'll be starting my presentation in five minutes. If you're interested in seeing a rare bird in its natural habitat, please come find a seat."

For no other reason except he happened to be standing nearby the stage with a wry smile, I caught a man's odd reaction to Nora's announcement. The thirty something man, tall with a husky build and a bird watcher's khaki, multi-pocketed vest, laughed dryly as Nora finished. He was leaning against a corner wall near the stage. His arrogant nose flare only added to the derisive laugh. It seemed he and Nora knew each other, and they were not friends. She ignored him and his mean laugh entirely as she shuffled through her note cards.

Half of the seats were taken, and they were filling up fast.

Elsie looked at me. "Who knew so many people were interested in bird pictures."

CHAPTER 8

$\mathcal{E}$lsie and I had spotted our seats for Nora's slideshow. It was just a matter of sidling past the legs of some of the people sitting, but our quest was stopped before we'd even reached the row of seats.

"Elsie," someone called from behind. We spun around. Minnie was walking quickly our way, her ample hips swinging side to side, as she hurried toward us. A forty-something man of medium height and build with dark hair and deep set eyes seemed to be walking alongside her, his longer legs allowing for a much less harried pace.

Minnie was somewhat winded by the time she reached us. "Oh, Elsie, I'm so glad you haven't left yet." Her cheeks rounded like apples. "I wanted to introduce you to the president of our club, Andrew Teslow." She beamed as if she was introducing a truly important person.

Andrew nodded. "So you're the marvelous baker of the famous dove cookies." He smiled politely and shook Elsie's hand. Then he smiled at me.

"Hello, I'm Lacey. I would like to take credit for the famous cookies, but I only helped deliver them."

He shook my hand regardless. "Nice to meet you." He turned back to Elsie. "Your cookies are so popular, I wanted to thank you in person. Also, since your cookies are so delicious, I assume you probably bake a stellar batch of brownies."

"Beyond stellar," I piped up before Elsie could answer. "Sorry, it's just I've been treated to many of her brownies, and stellar is not quite a big enough word to describe them."

"Perfect," Andrew said cheerfully. "Is there any way I can order three dozen of your brownies for our club picnic? It's tomorrow."

While Elsie calculated her time to see if she could manage the order on short notice, I decided to scoot between the rows of chairs and grab two seats before they filled up. I scooted along and as I brushed a curl back from my cheek, I caught the distinctive scent of orange. With my nose being as discerning as it was, I was almost sure it was the same orange that Minnie had been eating, or at least of the same variety. Since I hadn't eaten an orange and I'd washed my hands before and after the potato, I could only assume the orange scent came from Andrew's hand. Wherever it came from, I suddenly had an urge to eat an orange myself.

Some of the lights on the stage were being dimmed signaling that Nora was about to start. I headed toward a cluster of three empty chairs. I placed my purse on one chair to save it for Elsie and took a seat next to Ivy, the photographer.

Ivy leaned her head closer. "Glad to see you made it to the slideshow. Everyone has been waiting for this. Nora has been talking about it for months. She spotted it in a forest near the Canadian border."

"Yes, it'll be interesting to see," I said confidently as if I had any idea what a Goshawk was or why it would be rarely seen or, for that matter, living in a forest near Canada.

"Where is your friend?" Ivy asked.

Elsie was just making her way to the seat. "She's on her way." I patted the seat next to me. "She's a baker. The president of the bird watching society was asking her to bake some brownies for a club picnic."

"That's nice, I guess," she said hesitantly.

I looked at her. "Are brownies a bad idea for bird watchers?"

She laughed. "No, we like brownies well enough." It seemed she wasn't going to elaborate about her odd reaction to brownies at the picnic, then she huffed lightly. "I'm a member of the society. It's just that Andrew is always making spending decisions without going through the proper budget channels. Members have to vote on expenditures, but he is always veering off the list of approved expenses." She sighed loudly. "I guess that's why he's always having financial troubles in his personal life." She patted my arm. "But you didn't hear that from me."

"I won't say a word. But I will tell you that the brownies are delicious and will probably be the highlight of the picnic."

Elsie reached us right then. I picked up my purse so she could sit down, which she did with a clunk and a soft moan.

I glanced over at her. "Did you just make an old woman sound as you sat?" I couldn't hide my amusement. Elsie was the spriest, fittest person I knew and hearing her make a sound like my old Great Aunt Betty used to make when she sat at the Thanksgiving table was, to say the least, unusual.

"An old person sound escapes me once in awhile, and frankly, I deserve it. Now I've got to add three dozen brownies to my list for tomorrow."

I scrunched my face. "Should I not have told him they were beyond stellar?"

"No, no," she said. "After all, you were just telling the truth."

Nora had put up the first slide. It was a picture of her at a campsite somewhere in a lush green forest with a lake in the background. Inadvertently, I glanced across the room and found that the same guy with his arrogant grin and posture was standing near the stage. It seemed he planned to watch the slideshow from the side of the stage rather than with the audience.

I leaned my head toward Ivy. "Excuse me but is that man over there in the gray t-shirt with the short, reddish brown hair a member of your bird watching society?"

"Yes, that's Mason." She smiled. "Why are you interested? I could introduce you, but I have to warn you, a lot of women like him. I'm not sure why. He's very full of himself, and well, he's dishonest too but that's a long story."

"No, I'm not interested. He just looks sort of—" I paused, looking for the right words.

"Full of himself?" Ivy repeated.

"Yes, I guess that's it."

"Please, if I could have your attention." Nora's voice shot through the microphone. "I'd like to get started with my presentation."

Elsie elbowed me. "If I nod off, don't let me fall face first out of the chair. Did that once in college and nearly broke my nose."

"Just don't snore," I muttered back.

CHAPTER 9

*I*t was hard not to feel sorry for Nora Banks but then one also wondered why someone who obviously suffered from terrible stage fright would sign herself up for a presentation. And in front of her bird watching peers, no less.

Elsie was finding just a touch too much amusement with Nora's nervous presentation. The poor, frazzled woman dropped the microphone twice, mistaking it for the slide advance remote in her other hand. The second microphone drop caused the device to whistle slightly, so it sounded as if there was a perpetual gust of wind circling the auditorium. Twice, she used only her note cards as guides. Without looking up, she described a very nice image of a golden eagle, but the slide behind her was clearly a barn owl. (Even those of us with limited bird knowledge knew when we were looking at an owl and not an eagle.) All the while, arrogant looking Mason stood off to the side making no attempt to hide his derisive grin. Nora nervously glanced his direction more than once but she forged ahead.

"Two more slides," Nora said through the eerie whistle floating through the microphone, "and we'll reach the photo you've all been waiting for." She grasped for her pile of note cards, but rather than grabbing hold of them, her nervous fingers sent the cards cascading to the floor. A nice young man in the front row lunged out of his seat to help her collect them.

"This is starting to be sad," Elsie muttered. (She was still wearing an amused smile.)

I leaned toward her. "Starting? I can't believe anyone would put themselves through this."

Ivy apparently overheard my comment. "I'm not sure why she's so anxious," Ivy whispered. "I've seen her give presentations before, and she's usually great, relaxed and enjoying herself."

I glanced in the direction of the notoriously rude Mason. "Do you think it has something to do with your club mate, Mason?" I asked quietly. "He would make anyone anxious with his sardonic grin."

Ivy looked across the room at Mason. "He's always like that. Although, you might be right. Only, I think it might just be because Nora has been bragging about this photo for a long time, and now the time has come to put the picture behind her boasts. It's sort of the big reveal because I don't think anyone has seen it yet. I'm sure that's why Mason is here. He would never sit through a presentation by another club member. He thinks he knows everything."

There was definitely no love lost between Ivy and Mason.

Nora had collected her cards into a haphazard stack with corners sticking this way and that. She couldn't get them back in proper order, so she set them down with an exasperated sigh.

She ad-libbed through the next two slides and seemed to confuse a blue jay with a woodpecker. The whole presentation was mostly a disaster, so she just powered through the mistakes. Then, Nora became visibly more nervous. She wiped her palms on her pretty t-shirt as if they were sweaty, which judging by her agitated state was a given. Those of us in the audience were fidgeting as well, spurred into our own state of agitation by our presenter's unsteadiness.

"This is turning out to be more entertaining than I imagined," Elsie muttered behind her hand. "I'm half expecting her to throw up right in front of everyone."

Nora picked up the clicker to advance to the next slide, the apparent show piece of her presentation. There was an audible pause, as if someone pressed mute on the audience, as we waited for her to click over to the next slide.

"This bird must really be something," I said to Elsie from the side of my mouth.

Nora abruptly put the slide remote down on the projector cart. "You know, I'm not feeling too well. I think I need to end this presentation."

A loud groan of disappointment swallowed the stage area. The dull roar of frustration drew curious people from the rest of the auditorium toward the stage. Everyone wanted to find out what was going on.

I leaned over to Ivy. "Do you know Nora well? Maybe she could use some help right now," I suggested gently. "Before she passes out."

Ivy nodded. It seemed she was just about to get up when Mason, the arrogant looking man watching from the wings, spoke up. "No you don't, Nora." He strolled purposefully across to poor, trembling Nora. "You've been boasting about this photo for months, and we have a right to see it." His long arm reached past her. He grabbed the remote before she could stop him. (Not that she could, considering their difference in size and the fact that she looked ready to crumble into a million pieces.) His big thumb pressed the remote and the slide switched over to a beautiful scenic landscape sized photo of a hawk soaring over the tops of pine trees. Its belly was covered with pale blue-gray downy feathers and white fluff under its square tail. There were a few gasps in the audience. Ivy sat forward with interest but looked more puzzled than impressed.

Elsie leaned closer. "Looks like a regular old hawk to me."

"I don't think we have the expertise to tell the difference," I reminded her. "Just like many of the people in this audience would call a tart a small pie or a peony a fluffy carnation." I cut short my further analogies to watch the drama up front.

Mason had climbed up on stage to get closer to the screen. He stood in front of it, his back to us and hands on hips. Even the tautness of his shoulders exuded arrogance.

The audience had been lulled into a state of silent astonishment. No one seemed to know what was going on, especially those of us not involved with the West Coast Bird Watching Society. Nora was staring down at the ground. Her shoulders shook as if she was crying.

A cruel laugh bounced off the screen. Mason spun around and another even meaner laugh followed. He pointed up at the image behind him. "Does it look familiar?" he asked the audience.

"Yeah, it looks like every hawk I've ever seen," Elsie mumbled.

A low murmur began through the audience, and someone finally shouted what others were muttering. "That photo was taken fifty years ago by the great Alan Isop. That's Isop's Goshawk. It's just been enhanced."

More angry mumbles turned to shouting. "Nora, how could you deceive us like this?" someone asked.

Nora lifted her face. "I'm sorry. I did spot a Goshawk and I snapped a picture, but my camera broke before I could download it. I had a photo. I promise I had one. I had a change of heart. I knew it wasn't right. That's why I stopped the slideshow." She was in tears, but her face grew red with anger as she finally found the nerve to turn around and face the evil Mason, who was wearing the smirkiest smirk I'd ever seen.

She pointed a trembling finger at him. "You of all people have no right to cast stones. We all know that you won an award for someone else's photo. I hate you. Everyone hates you. Someday, I will laugh and spit on your grave!"

"And to think I was reluctant to attend this entertaining event," Elsie said. She could speak freely now due to the noise in the audience and the entire auditorium, for that matter. Most of the exchange had been picked up by the microphone on the projector cart. Onlookers were gathering to watch the horrible spectacle.

Two women up front mercifully got up and turned off the projector. One of the women took the microphone and announced that the presentation was over and that everyone should head over to the food area because all the vendors were offering twenty-five percent off for the rest of the night. That nice sale on all the goodies prompted people out of their chairs and toward the food area. Mason, apparently satisfied that he'd done all the humiliating damage he could possibly do for one evening, strode off the stage and off to wherever mean people went after they'd inflicted pain. The same two women who had turned off the projector and made the announcement walked Nora away from the stage area, consoling her with pats on the back and soft words.

Elsie stood up and stretched. "Well, that's probably enough of birds for the evening. What do you say we *fly* back home."

"I'm with you. Lots of ruffled feathers in this place."

CHAPTER 10

*T*he bizarre late afternoon at the bird event, thankfully, rolled into a lovely, quiet evening with my favorite detective and his adorable sidekick. I patted Bear's soft head as the dog curled up next to me on the sofa. He was far too big so his rear end and front end hung over the edge, but he was quite content to stay there. Briggs carried two bowls of rocky road ice cream out of his kitchen.

He rolled his eyes at his giant dog's attempt to imitate a cat curled on the couch. "I'm going to have to get a bigger couch." He handed me the bowl of ice cream.

"That's quite a change from your first proclamation after adding Bear to the family that he was not going to be allowed on furniture." I picked up the spoon and took a bite of the chocolaty treat.

"As you might recall, I tried that, but when he started teething and chewing the edges of the furniture that I was trying so hard to protect, I decided hairs on the cushions were better than three legged tables and armless couches." Briggs sat on the other side of me.

"As someone who has many a hairy couch cushion, I agree. Just don't wear black. That's a rule to live by when you have hairy furniture. On second thought, ignore that. I am particularly fond of you in black t-shirts. Gives you a sort of bad boy aura."

He laughed over a mouthful of rocky road. "That's what I strive for, after all. Aside from the strange afternoon at the bird convention, how did the rest of the work day go with the new assistant?"

We both settled into the cushions with our bowls of ice cream.

"Let's just say things didn't get better as far as her relationship with Kingston. She took the initiative to send him outside . . . with a broom."

Briggs sat forward and looked at me. "So you fired her?"

I took a deep breath. "No and I feel sort of traitorous to my bird, but he was fine. He went over to console himself with bakery crumbs. She didn't touch him with the broom. She just used it to shoo him outside. I told her that I was the only person who could let him outside. She seemed to understand that I was upset. But I need her. I've got three weddings this month. I can't do the arrangements alone. Am I a terrible bird mom?" I'd had plenty of guilt lumps in my stomach since the afternoon. If I wasn't in such desperate need of a floral assistant, I would have sent Barbara on her way.

Briggs rested back. "No, you're not a bad bird mom. In fact, some might say you're just a little too doting of a mom. You spoil that crow. Like you said, he was fine and you need Barbara's help. It does make me wonder whether or not I want a new partner. I'm definitely overwhelmed with the amount of work I have, but a new partner might just be more work and more trouble."

"It would be nice if you had help," I said. "They stretch you way too thin."

"True. There's been a lull in big cases for the past month. I have to admit it's been great catching up on paperwork. Maybe we'll get lucky and float through the whole summer without any murders or big crimes."

I turned my face and stared at him.

He nodded. "Yes, you're right. I should never have said that out loud." He leaned forward and rapped his knuckles on the coffee table. "Speaking of murders—" he continued after he leaned back. "What did Marty have for you?"

"Oh wow, it's been such an eventful day, I nearly forgot all about my wonderful lunch with Marty. We were, of course, given the star treatment with a mountain of crispy fries and that nice table that doesn't get too much sun or too much noise from the kitchen. It's Marty's regular table. I wouldn't be surprised if Franki saw Marty coming across the parking lot and yanked customers off the table so that she could give it to Marty. It was ready for us when we walked inside."

Briggs laughed. "Marty definitely has a fan club in this town."

"I'm certainly part of that club. I brought the photo he gave me." I stood from the couch, disturbing Bear from his nap. He decided it was time to get off the couch and stretch, particularly if I was heading to the kitchen and near his treat jar. He poured his large, fuzzy body languidly off the couch and dropped right down into a doggie stretch with his massive paws out front and his rear high in the air. I circled around Bear with the two empty ice cream bowls. I carried them to the kitchen sink, grabbed a treat from the jar and stopped by my purse for the photo of Jane Price.

"Remember that I found those love letters to Teddy from Button in Bertram's trunk?" I reminded Briggs as I tossed the cookie to Bear and sat back down on the couch.

"Yes, the ones with the lavender. You thought they might have been from someone other than Mrs. Bertram, someone like Jane Price."

"Exactly and now I no longer have to theorize. I have proof." I handed him the photo. "This is Jane Price, but the interesting part is on the back." I continued as Briggs turned the yellowed photo over. "Marty isn't sure why his mom had the photo in her collection, but clearly, Jane had meant to give it someone she referred to as Teddy."

"To Teddy from Button," Briggs read. He smiled at me. "Good detective work, Miss Pinkerton."

"Thank you, although this one sort of landed in my lap. Right over the plate of crispy fries. But there's more. I put some puzzle pieces together. I have no doubt that Bertram fathered Jane's baby. Remember that monthly withdrawal of seventy-three dollars from Bertram's account after Jane left town? The withdrawal that had no notation with it?"

"Yes, that's right. So Bertram was paying for Jane's room and board and possibly even medical care. I suppose seventy-three dollars would have gone a long way back then."

"I'd say so, and back then women didn't have much access to *manly* things such as account ledgers. I'm sure Jill Hawksworth had no idea family funds were being diverted to a pregnant mistress. Or maybe she knew and just kept quiet so as to keep the scandal from being blown about town. Either way, it's all very intriguing. I can't wait to find out more."

Briggs put his arm around my shoulder and drew me closer. "It seems to me you're getting close to the truth. I must admit, I can't wait either. It will certainly stir things up in this town if it turns out there was a lot more to the tragedy than a despondent patriarch deciding to take out his entire family before turning the gun on himself. If it's true that Bertram Hawksworth was a victim and not the culprit, then it's only fair that, after all this time, his name is cleared."

"I agree." That thought took me back to the feelings of trepidation that reared their pointy heads every time I considered how some of my more prominent theories might pan out. Mayor Price already disliked me in every possible way and for every possible reason. I could only imagine how his negative feelings would grow tenfold if I implicated his great-grandfather in the terrible murders. But my intuition was telling me, and strongly, that Mayor Harvard Price had some hand or knew some details about the crime.

Briggs sensed that I'd been drawn into one of my worrisome thoughts. He squeezed me again. "Everything all right?"

"Yes, everything is fine. I was just visualizing Mayor Price's red face and flaring nostrils when I uncover a horrible secret about his great-grandfather."

"So you still think there's a connection between the Hawksworth murders and Harvard Price?"

I sighed deeply. "Yep and this time I don't even need Samantha's help." I tapped my powerful nose. "This time I'm going to find the killer without one out of place smell or one handsome detective."

CHAPTER 11

*B*arbara was early. She waited outside the flower shop with Amelia. They spoke to each other briefly as Kingston and I walked toward the shop door. They didn't seem to be striking up any kind of a friendship, which was not too surprising. Amelia seemed somewhat traumatized by the whole broom incident. It made me like her even more. Barbara, on the other hand, did not score any points by scowling disapprovingly at Kingston as we neared.

It was a beautiful morning, and I quickly decided it might be in everyone's best interest, crow included, if I sent Kingston off for a little jaunt around town. He was only too happy to oblige and hardly needed one word from me before trotting down the sidewalk and lifting off to perch in one of his favorite trees. It was a flowering plum tree that gave him a perfectly unobstructed view of Lola's Antiques. Not that he had any interest in Victorian sideboards or Chippendale mirrors. On second thought, my vain bird did love a good mirror, but his keen interest in my friend's shop had to do with its owner.

Amelia knew all about Kinston's crush. She spun back around after watching Kingston find his morning tree perch. "I'll bet he's waiting for Lola to get to her shop. That poor guy has it bad," she said with a head shake.

Barbara had no comment to add. She held her purse in one hand and a lunch bag in the other. I could only imagine how neatly her lunch was arranged inside the canvas tote, pickles in their own little container and orange slices already peeled and ready to consume.

"I'm looking forward to putting together the white orchid, orange rose bouquets," Barbara said as I unlocked the door. "I love working with orchids."

And that, I thought to myself, was why I needed her. I found orchids to be too delicate and stubborn. The door opened and I waved my two assistants inside. Before I took my own step into the shop, a car screeched to a halt in front of Les's coffee. I glanced back and saw a very angry Nora Banks climbing out of a small, blue sedan. She was pointing at a person who was apparently sitting at Les's outdoor tables. I couldn't see the table area without stepping out onto the sidewalk.

"You, you jerk," Nora spat. "I hope you get attacked by a thousand crows just like the Hitchcock movie." She tripped and stumbled forward in her rage, but she managed to catch herself. A harsh, cruel laugh rolled out from the table area. I recognized it instantly, and suddenly, Nora's anger made sense.

Not deterred by Mason's callous response, Nora marched toward him on hiking boots. She was still waving her finger at him and telling him all the ways she'd like to see him suffer. Although none as colorful as the Hitchcock movie idea. Had she gotten the idea from the big black bird glowering down at the her from his flowering plum branch? It seemed likely.

I handed my purse inside. "Amelia, could you put this in the office? I think Les might need my help next door. I'll be right there."

I closed the shop door and circled around to the table area. As I expected, Les had come out to see what the commotion was about. Nora was still in a rant, waving her arms and letting Mason know that he was the worst person in the world. Naturally, he just sat there with a smug smile, which even I felt like wiping off his face.

Les was offering Nora a free coffee if she came inside. He saw me and mouthed the word 'help'.

"Hello, Nora, I don't know if you remember me. I own the flower shop next door." I spoke calmly hoping she could hear me somewhere in her rage filled haze.

"This man is a monster. Someone needs to do something about him." Her tone was less sharp, but her face was still red.

"You caused your own problems," Mason sneered before taking a sip of his coffee. "She got caught up in her own scam," he explained. Neither of them had any idea that I was in the audience the night before and that I had witnessed the entire debacle. He shrugged. "All I did was expose her for being a fraud."

"You're the fraud," Nora screamed just as a couple arrived at the coffee shop. They looked concerned and turned around, apparently deciding to get their morning coffee elsewhere. Les looked pleadingly at me.

Mason certainly wasn't helping. He sat there and nonchalantly sipped his coffee as if he didn't have a care in the world.

"Les, why don't you bring one of your special summer hibiscus teas over to the shop for Nora."

Nora heard her name and glanced at Les and me as if noticing us for the first time. She had been so consumed by anger, she seemed almost puzzled to see us.

"Nora," I said politely, "let's go next door. You can sit and relax and have one of Les's fabulous iced teas."

She hesitated but only for a second. "Actually, that's a good idea.

I need to get away from this viper and cool down." She cast Mason a scowl that could curl toes. He continued sipping coffee.

I breathed a sigh of relief as I led her away from the Coffee Hutch and over to Pink's Flowers. Naturally, Amelia and Barbara were slightly astonished that I was leading someone into the store, and particularly a person who was clearly distressed.

"Barbara, if you want to go ahead and get started with the bouquets, I'll join you in just a few minutes. Amelia, if you don't mind, could you walk over to Les's and pick up the hibiscus tea he's preparing for Miss Banks."

Nora's face shot my direction. "How do you know my name?"

I nodded toward my assistants, and they headed off to their tasks.

"Why don't you sit first." I pointed out one of the stools at the work island.

Nora sat on a stool and glanced over at Kingston's empty perch. "Your crow? Did he fly away?"

"No, he's just out for some morning exercise. He'll be back soon."

A look of disapproval crossed her face. "Are you sure he wouldn't be happier being free?"

I had to bite my tongue, considering the woman had gone through a humiliating ordeal the night before. Her subsequent anger filled attack on a fellow club member was probably only going to add to her humiliation.

"I'm sure," I said curtly to assure her that Kingston was not going to be discussed. I decided to redirect her away from my life and back to hers. "You asked why I knew your last name," I reminded her. "I was at the bird convention last night."

An unexpected smile appeared. "That's right. I talked you into attending." The smile vanished as it dawned on her what that meant in terms of me knowing all about her slideshow fiasco.

Amelia returned almost instantly with the dark pink glass of tea. Nora gladly accepted the drink and took a few refreshing sips. "This is just what I needed. Thank you so much. I suppose you saw the entire, horrid nightmare last night."

"I did. I'm sorry that it happened. But maybe it's best if you just stay clear of Mason. He seems rather—"

"Cruel? Arrogant? Unlikable? He's all those things plus dishonest. No one likes him. He has one friend, John Jacobs, but John is friends with everyone. He's the opposite of Mason."

"Why is Mason allowed to stay a member?" I asked.

"He's a big contributor. Frankly, I think it's because people are afraid of him. He's mean and vindictive. He likes to humiliate people, so members try and stay on his good side."

I shook my head. "Sounds like a typical schoolyard bully. Well, I hope you're feeling better now."

Nora finished another long sip and breathed a sigh. "Yes, this cold drink helps, and if I'm honest about it, I feel better after yelling at him. Not even sure of the things I said, but it was therapeutic. Even if he just sat smugly through it all."

I smiled. "There was a mention of crows attacking him like in a Hitchcock movie, which I thought was rather creative."

Nora laughed. "I think I spotted a crow in a tree, and that put the idea in my head. I suddenly visualized Mason running from a murder of crows as they swooped at him, pecking at his head and face." She pulled her mouth tight. "I'm not usually that ghoulish, but Mason brings out the worst in people, including me."

Barbara rolled out the cart with all the flowers we needed for the bouquets.

"Those are beautiful," Nora said. "It must be wonderful working around flowers all day." She slipped down off the stool. "I'll let you get to work. I can see you're very busy."

"Wait," I said. "I'll peek around the corner and make sure Mason is gone."

"Would you? That's so kind. I know seeing him would just stir me up again."

"No problem." I headed outside and glanced around. No sign of Mason or my bird. I walked back inside. "Coast is clear."

Nora hurried past. "Thanks again."

"Have a great day."

CHAPTER 12

J sensed by the way Lola's short black boots thudded the shop floor that she was upset about something. She climbed onto a stool like a sloth, with slow, heavy movements. With Lola, a dour mood could mean anything from an aggravating call with her mother to a sandwich with a flavorless tomato. What I didn't know was that the reason for her sour mood was going to be equally upsetting for me.

Barbara had taken her brown bag lunch to the town square, and Amelia was entering purchase orders on my computer. There were no customers, so Lola and I had the shop to ourselves.

"Why so glum?" I asked. "Did they forget the pickle at the sandwich shop?"

"If only my woes had to do with trivial things like pickles. Nope, this is truly bad news, and you better brace yourself too. Ryder and I were chatting on Skype, and he dropped a bomb."

I sucked in and held a breath to wait for the *bomb*.

"He's staying an extra three weeks. He won't be home until August." With that proclamation, she dropped her forehead onto the island.

I released the breath. I was feeling some of her pain since that meant another three weeks with Barbara as my floral assistant. The otherwise productive morning had been marred by Barbara fussing and fidgeting with every one of my bouquets and with the return of Kingston from his morning adventure. Barbara kept eyeing him suspiciously as if she feared he might swoop over and attack her. It seemed the Hitchcock movie was on everyone's minds today.

"We've survived this long," I said. "We can make it a little longer. How is he doing? Is he well? Is he enjoying himself?"

Lola sat up and shrugged. "Not sure. I sort of shut down mentally after he told me the devastating news."

"Ryder staying an extra three weeks could hardly be categorized as devastating." I began picking up the floral and ribbon remnants of our morning bouquet creation.

"Easy for you to say—your boyfriend will be in town all summer. Ryder and I are missing out on beach picnics, bike rides and watching summer sunsets."

"OK, first of all, you aren't big on any of those common romantic activities. When was the last time you took a bike ride?"

Her shoulders slumped wrinkling the Pink Floyd logo on the front of her t-shirt. "Well, if I did want to take one with my boyfriend, that would be impossible because he's a gazillion miles away in some hot, sticky forest with bugs and probably some statuesque, curvy woman scientist who wears thick rimmed black glasses that make her look smart as well as sexy."

"Now you're just being silly."

Lola looked around at the empty shop front. "Where's the new floral arranger? Hope she's good because your usual arranger is probably going to run off with his smart and sexy team member to live in some exotic location where the flowers grow in the garden instead of in glass vases."

A laugh shot from my mouth. "You do realize that the flowers in our vases actually came from a garden, right? And Ryder will be back soon. He's not running off with anyone."

Kingston had come back so tired from his morning adventure, it had taken until that time for him to work up the energy to drop down from his perch, march across the floor and fly up to the empty stool next to Lola.

"Who cares if Ryder does run off with another woman." Lola reached over and rubbed Kingston's head. "I've got my loyal guy right here. You would never desert me for a pretty parrot would ya, King?"

The door opened and Elsie walked in.

"Thank goodness." I tilted my head toward Lola. "This one is crazier than usual today."

"That's it." Lola hopped off the stool. "I'm withdrawing my nomination from the Greatest Best Friend contest. I'm heading back to my shop with the dusty old things and the creepy Victorian garden gnomes my mom just sent from Ireland. I hate when she sends things with eyes. Goodbye." She swept out of the shop without a glance back.

Elsie raised her brow in question.

"Ryder's staying an extra three weeks," I said.

"Oh boy. That means another three weeks of her moping and another three weeks of—" She motioned to the hallway and lifted her brows again.

I shook my head. "It's just Amelia. Barbara went to lunch."

"Is she still fixing all your arrangements?" she whispered.

"She sure is. But enough about my fun. I noticed you arrived empty handed, so you're not looking for a taste tester. What's up?"

"I need your help. Do you have a lot more to do this afternoon?" She rubbed Kingston's head.

"Thanks to the very efficient Barbara, my orders are finished. Why do you ask?"

"Minnie has asked if I could deliver the brownies for the picnic.

They're eating lunch in Mayfield Park near the beach. I don't have two assistants," she said as if I was spoiled rotten with help.

"That's because you choose not to," I reminded her.

"It's not a choice. It's a matter of keeping my sanity." She switched to a fake, sweet smile. "Do you think you could deliver them for me? There's a free muffin in it for you."

"I already get muffins free from you, which, of course means I owe you, so yes, I'll deliver your brownies. I'm curious to see what's going on with the bird watchers anyhow. Did Les tell you about his morning?"

Elsie shook her head, then seemed to recall it. "That's right. I guess I only half listen when Les is talking, but he said something about an angry woman telling a man she wished crows would peck out his eyes."

I chuckled. "Yes, well that does sound like a Les version. I don't know if she was quite so graphic in her threat, but needless to say, it was quite the scene. But the part that will interest you is that the woman was Nora, the woman with the humiliating slideshow, and Mason, the awful guy who exposed her scam was the target of her rage."

Elsie's eyes rounded. "Oh wow, I can't believe I missed that. Did she give it to him good?"

"She gave it her best, but it was not a great scene for the coffee shop. Poor Les was anxious to end the drama. He gave her a free tea, and I walked her over here to the flower shop to cool down . . . in every way. I'll deliver those brownies and see how it's going at the picnic. Should be interesting. I'll be over as soon as Barbara returns from lunch."

"Sounds good. I'll get them all packed up."

"Save a broken one for the delivery girl," I called as she walked out of the shop.

CHAPTER 13

The park in Mayfield was a lush twenty plus acres of
forest, complete with crude dirt trails and the occasional large rock or wooden bench to sit on. One side of the park
was bordered by a parking lot, restrooms and a dozen picnic
tables. The far side of the park ended where the beach, rocks and
ocean began. It was a scenic mix of forest and coast.

Three dozen brownies produced an overwhelming chocolaty
scent, particularly for my nose. I was nearly dizzy from the rich
cocoa fragrance as I parked the car in the lot. A long white
passenger van was parked across three spots. The words West
Coast Bird Watching Society were emblazoned across its side in
bright blue letters. A large banner with the club name billowed like
a ship's sail as it hung between two trees. There were small clusters
of people talking and eating lunch. Andrew, the club president,
was standing at the head of one of the tables talking to a group of
people who were raptly listening to him as they sipped cold sodas.
I only scanned the area briefly, but I didn't spot Mason or Nora in
the crowd.

I leaned into the backseat of my car and pulled out the massive box of brownies. Naturally, Elsie had frosted them thickly with her famous chocolate butter cream. She had even taken the time to add a delicate yellow frosting flower to each treat. The broken bits she'd given me for the ride to Mayfield were gooey and delicious.

Andrew glanced up long enough from his talk to spot me heading across the lot with the brownies. He said something to one of the women at the table, and she immediately hopped up and headed my direction. It was Ivy. She was wearing a stylish pair of shorts and dark brown lace up boots that ended just above the ankles. She hurried over with a big smile and was surprised to see me.

"Oh, it's you again. How interesting that we keep meeting." She reached for the box. "Here, I'll take those. They smell delicious. I wish I could have one."

I handed her the box. "You're not going to try one of Elsie's brownies? You're going to be missing out on a treat."

She leaned closer and whispered even though we were still a good distance from the tables. "I don't eat gluten. It bloats me."

My nose twitched as it sensed something other than chocolate. "Is that pine I'm smelling?" I asked.

Her mouth dropped open for a second. "How on earth did you smell that? I was sitting in one of those tall pines at the end of the first trail. Sometimes the best camera shots are taken from the branch of a tree." She moved her nose to smell her shoulder. "I didn't realize that I left that tree smelling like Christmas."

"It's probably not that strong. It's just that I have a really powerful nose." We crossed the gravel lot to the picnic area.

"By the way," Ivy was whispering again. It seemed our neighboring seats at the slideshow had pushed us into a semi-friendship, one close knit enough for whispering 'by the ways'. "You might notice one of our members is conspicuously absent," she continued in a hushed tone. "Nora decided to go off on her own adventure.

She sat for a sandwich and then hurried away. Can't say I blame her. Especially because Mason is at the picnic."

"No, I can't blame her either."

Andrew nodded to his little audience and walked over to greet us. "We've been anxious for these brownies. We're all hungry from a long morning of bird watching." He took hold of the box.

"Did you spot anything interesting?" I asked, only my question was drowned out by someone yelling. It was a frantic, scared sound that sent a group of us running into the woods. Two women, both in club shirts, were standing near a large shrub consoling each other. They looked pale and horrified.

"Here," was all the first woman could say as she pointed shakily to something behind the shrub.

Their looks of horror were enough to keep the others, Andrew included, from checking out the point of interest. Something told me it wasn't just going to be a dead sparrow. I circled around the shrub. Ivy and two of the men followed but hesitantly. I spotted the hiking boots first, then the long pair of legs covered to mid calf in gray socks and mid thigh in cargo shorts, but the rest of the body was hidden beneath glossy green leaves of the sprawling Pacific Wax Myrtle bush. Some of the plant's purple berries had stained the olive green cargo shorts. He was on his back as if just napping under a shrub

"Good lord," one of the men, an elderly man with a straw hat and binoculars hanging around his neck ushered in a shocked tone. "That's Mason. I believe that's Mason Fanning. I saw him in those shorts this morning."

"Is he dead?" Ivy asked. Her question sounded almost too enthusiastic considering the content *and* context. She also, noticeably, appeared far less shocked than the others. Even the club president stood back with the others, seemingly petrified to come forward.

My intuition and short experience in medical school told me I was looking at the lower half of a dead body, but I was no expert. I hoped my intuition was wrong as I tread carefully next to his limp hand and parted the fragrant waxy leaves. It was indeed Mason Fanning. A massive stain of blood covered the left side of his chest. It was easy to spot the source of the blood, a large gash. Without closer inspection, I could only guess that it was caused by a knife or a bullet shot at close range. His face was tilted toward me. The grayish tint of his skin and slightly open stare of his eyes assured me he was dead. But I was in no position to say so.

I looked back at the club members, all waiting anxiously to hear what I had to say. "Please call the police and tell them we need an ambulance."

"So he's still alive?" Andrew asked, shakily from the other side of the bush. "Thank goodness," he said.

It wasn't my place to break the bad news or give any official word on Mason's condition, and I had no gloves on hand to take his pulse. I was certain I wouldn't find one.

The man with the straw hat took off his binoculars and handed them to Ivy. "Let's pull him out from the bush." He reached for Mason's ankles.

"Wait." I put up my hand.

I didn't want the crime scene compromised, but now I had to go along with the ruse that poor Mason was still alive. Naturally, the first thing one would do was pull him free from the shrub. I needed to come up with a good reason to leave him shoved beneath the bush. Everyone stared at me with wide eyes waiting for me to continue. An idea popped into my head.

"There is some bleeding." I hoped the word *some* would make it all sound less alarming, but there was a good round of gasps anyhow. "I'm worried that if we move him it will hasten the blood flow."

"Yes, and what if he hurt his back," someone in the group said.

"Exactly," I said briskly. "We don't want to injure him more."

"The ambulance is on its way," someone yelled.

I needed to get word to Briggs about the severity of the situation. I pulled my phone out. I knew I wasn't going to be able to talk to him without curious, worried ears tuning in, so I sent off a brief text and tried to make it as clear as possible.

"I'm at Mayfield Park, near the beach, and there is a body. Pretty sure a dead one, but I didn't want to alarm the bystanders so an ambulance is on its way." I pressed send and hoped he wasn't in a meeting or at the courthouse.

A text pinged right back. "What is it with you and dead bodies? Be right there."

I was relieved. I'd also been so distracted, I hadn't noticed that Mr. Straw Hat had taken it upon himself to check on Mason. His rather rotund bottom half was sticking out of the shrub, and the top half had disappeared inside.

"Please, leave him—" I started, but it was too late.

His top half emerged, fast enough that the shrub grabbed hold of the straw hat. "I think he's dead!" he yelled. "There's blood everywhere."

A bundle of screams and gasps and horrified looks followed.

The man stumbled back, away from the shrub. I lunged forward to keep him from collapsing. His gray eyes clashed with mine. He quickly and astutely understood why I'd kept the whole terrible thing on the down low. "You didn't want to upset everyone," he said in a low hoarse voice. "I'm sorry."

But it was too late. Word spread quickly, faster than the ambulances and police. Soon everyone in Mayfield Park knew there was a dead man in the shrubs.

CHAPTER 14

*M*ayfield Park's rather obscure location between forest and coastline made it a harder place to reach. Ambulances and police cars would have to travel along a stretch of dirt road followed by a gravel driveway. It delayed their arrival just long enough for me to snoop around before the *officials* took over.

Andrew, who had the lofty position of president, was fairly useless during the entire crisis. He stood frozen in a stunned stupor even as some of the others were coming around to the bleak reality.

Ivy seemed to be holding it together well, almost too well. It seemed she was no fan of Mason's. She was consoling a few of the others as they meandered aimlessly around the crime scene. I worried they would disturb evidence. I rushed over to Ivy.

"Ivy, the emergency crews will be here soon. We need someone to meet them at the parking lot and lead them to this area. It would be especially helpful if this whole section of trail was cleared and free of hikers. Most of these people look quite stricken. Perhaps a brownie would help."

Ivy nodded. "Right. I can help with that. I'll clear the area." She hopped right into action and seemed to have the confidence and respect of the others, so they followed her instructions and shuffled warily back toward the picnic benches. Fortunately, the crime scene was out of view of the picnic area.

I walked back to the victim and knelt down beside him to do a preliminary smell check. After working with a horticulture expert like Ryder, I knew that the shrub Mason's body had fallen in was a fragrant bird favorite. The leaves were occasionally used in place of bay leaves. The shrub was certainly fragrant like bay but not so strong that it masked the other obvious plant smell—pine. Of course, we were surrounded by pine trees and every form of evergreen, but this particular whiff of pine was more concentrated. Like the scent I smelled on Ivy as I met her in the parking lot.

Since the area had been thankfully cleared, I took the liberty to lean over Mason's body and give it a good sniff. The blood was drying but still overwhelming. I twitched my nose to try and get the acrid, metallic smell out of my olfactory cells. Certain odors were more easily dismissed than others. Unfortunately, blood, especially in copious amounts, did not fall into that category.

Still, I managed to find some heavily concentrated patches of fresh pine. Ivy had mentioned that she was perched in a pine tree waiting for a good shot. Had Mason used the same technique of tree sitting?

While I continued my nose survey, I couldn't help but think back to the morning when Nora threatened him with bird attacks and other creative dangers. She had gone through something horribly humiliating. Was she angry enough to kill Mason? It sure seemed that way at the coffee shop.

My main take away from the nasal inspection was pine. It was hardly an odd smell for the location, but I wondered how Mason got so much of it on his clothes. In the distance, siren screams were being lifted away from their sources and distributed into the ocean air. It was hard to get a sense of how close they were, but my time was limited. Since I'd had the grim privilege of discovering the dead body, it seemed only right that I got first crack at the evidence.

I glanced around, then my eyes swept down across Mason's boots. His feet rested in a dried pile of forest debris, but directly in front of the heels were two channels where the debris had been cleared to the rich, loamy soil beneath. My gaze followed the two, long divots, and I quickly discovered two thin trails through the debris. It seemed someone had dragged Mason's lifeless body across forest floor. The killer might have thought they could hide his body but, apparently, underestimated the victim's size or overestimated the width and depth of the shrub. The concentrated pine smell was beginning to make sense. A good portion of the litter on the forest floor was fallen pine needles. I followed the fairly easy to spot heel trail about fifty feet across the clearing to a large pine tree. My shoe tapped something in the fallen needles.

I stooped down and carefully brushed away some of the dried needles, taking care not to touch the object beneath. A pair of binoculars was nestled into the debris. Its leather strap was broken away from the binoculars on one side. It seemed Mason might have struggled to get away from his attacker.

Voices pulled me from my thoughts. I pushed to my feet and headed back to the trail to meet up with Briggs. I had plenty to tell him. Halfway along the trail left by the heels of Mason's boots, a flash of red caught my eye. I glanced down and spotted a bright red feather sticking out of some dead leaves. I had never seen anything like it. I wondered what kind of bird it belonged to. I leaned down and picked it up. It felt soft and silky in my fingers as I pushed it gently into the pocket of my shorts.

Detective James Briggs was the first person to emerge from the curtain of evergreen. He was followed closely by two paramedics, both carrying their heavy gear, none of it necessary. Two Mayfield police officers followed behind the paramedics.

Briggs spotted Mason's boots before I had a chance to point out the shrub. He circled the bush and immediately parted the branches to get a good look at the upper torso and head. He disappeared almost entirely into the glossy green foliage for a good minute, then reappeared wearing latex gloves and a grim expression. He shook his head at the paramedics, but they'd already figured they weren't going to be needed. They turned around and trekked back, heavy bags and all, toward the parking area.

I waited patiently while Briggs briefly gave instructions for evidence collection and told one of the attending officers to make sure no one entered the trail area. He made a quick call to the coroner's office, then put away his phone and pulled out his notebook.

There was a glimmer of affection in his brown eyes as he approached me and straightened into his official posture. "Well, Pinkerton, it seems you have stumbled upon another murder scene. A fatal stabbing, if my first guess is right." He motioned for me to follow him a few feet away from where the action was about to take place. "Have you found out who the victim is?" he asked.

"Didn't need to find out. I already knew. His name is Mason Fanning, and he's a member of the West Coast Bird Watching Society. They're in town for the bird convention. Would you like to know more?" I asked with a bright smile.

He pulled out his pen. "Of course."

"Now, I'm just an amateur investigator, of course," I said pointedly, "but my guess would be that Mason was attacked and stabbed over by that big pine tree. Then the killer dragged his body across the trail to that shrub. I think they were hoping to hide his body completely, but as you see, Mason is a big man." I pointed out the two nearly parallel drag lines through the forest debris and showed him how they stopped at the heels of Mason's boots.

Briggs surveyed everything as he walked to the pine tree.

"Watch out for the pair of binoculars," I said from behind. "They are sort of half buried under the tree. It looks as if the strap had been broken in some sort of struggle."

Briggs stopped and stared down at the pair of binoculars. He pulled out his phone and took a picture before crouching down and touching some of the debris with his gloved fingers. He lifted his hand and rubbed smears of blood between two fingers.

"I think your theory was right," he said. "Mr. Fanning was stabbed right here under this tree. Then his attacker dragged him toward the shrub, hoping to hide the body." He pushed up to standing. There was the slightest glint of pride in his faint smile. He always worked hard to stay stony faced and professional at a murder scene, but I knew him well enough to detect even the slightest show of emotion.

"Is that all you know about our victim?" he asked. "Or do you know where I should start with the interviews?"

I shrugged shyly. "Oh . . . I might know where to start."

CHAPTER 15

*A*fter some more detailed instruction to the evidence team, Briggs had time to hear details about the dynamics between the group members before the coroner and his team arrived.

Briggs stood with pen in hand ready to write down information. It was cute and kind of impractical.

"I've got sort of a long story." I hopped up on tiptoes and peered over at his notepad. "Not sure if you'll be able to fit it all on your little detective pad."

"Fine, Miss Sarcasm, just tell me the important parts, and I'll try to summarize."

"All right but summaries are not my strong suit. Here goes. The first person you'll want to talk to is Nora Banks."

He jotted down her name and put a star by it. "See, my little notebook works just fine."

I chuckled behind my hand. "All right. Remember last night when I told you I went to the big bird convention they're having in the Mayfield Auditorium, and I told you there was a whole drama thing but I wasn't in the mood to relay details. Well, now I think I better tell you the details because Mason Fanning was involved in the drama and so was—" I pointed to the name on his pad. "Nora Banks. Nora was putting on a much anticipated presentation. Apparently, for months she had been boasting to her fellow bird watchers that she had captured a rare image of a Goshawk, in flight no less."

Briggs blinked his heavy dark lashes at me. "A what?"

I waved my hand. "A Goshawk. It's a type of hawk."

"That part I figured out on my own."

"Anyhow, it's a bird that is rarely photographed, and so it was a big deal. Only Nora didn't really capture the image. It turned out she stole an old image from a photographer who had actually captured a picture of the real thing. Poor Nora seemed to have a terrible case of guilt before she showed the slide. She shut down the presentation." I shook my head. "I thought she might just pass out from nerves. Well, Mason Fanning"—I pointed back over my shoulder in case Briggs forgot who Mason was—"Mason had been standing in the wings, off stage, with what I could only describe as a condescending, arrogant, smug grin."

Briggs had been scribbling quickly in his notebook. He paused and looked up at me. "I'll just put smug."

"I guess that's all right. Mason was not going to let Nora get away without showing the slide she'd been bragging about for months. He lumbered over to the stage and flipped on the slide. He just as quickly reminded the audience where the original photo had come from. Nora left in complete and utter despair. Humiliated in front of all her bird watching peers."

"Sounds like Nora is a good place to start." Briggs flipped the page. "Anyone else?"

"There is a woman named Ivy." I tapped my chin. "Let me think. Her last name was comically appropriate." I snapped my fingers. "That's right. Eagleton. Ivy Eagleton. She was one of the few brave people who was at my side when the women who discovered the body screamed. I must say, she was more than brave. The sight of a dead body, no matter how hidden in a shrub, didn't seem to upset her at all. Especially considering she knew the victim. Not that she had any love for the man." I crinkled my nose. "He was not a likable guy, and according to Nora, Mason wasn't liked by too many people."

He bunched his dark brows. "So you've already spoken to Nora? Lacey, you—"

"Hold off on the lecture, Detective. This was all before any body was found. Nora spotted Mason sipping coffee at Les's tables this morning. She jumped out of her car to give him an earful of what she thought of him. She had a lot to say on that matter, but I led her into the flower shop to calm her down. That's when she told me no one liked Mason."

Right then, a perfectly timed groan of anguish rolled toward us. A thirty-something tall, lean and well-groomed man had somehow gotten past the police. He stood near the body and braced his hands against his thighs to catch his breath.

"Looks as if at least someone liked him," Briggs said. He pushed the notebook into his coat pocket. "Let's find out who he is."

"I think his name is John Jacobs."

Briggs stopped and looked at me. "How on earth—"

"What can I say—I'm like a fly on the wall in everyone's lives."

He shook his head and continued toward the bereaved man. "If I didn't know any better, I'd think you've secretly been a member of the West Coast Bird Watching Society."

I skipped a few paces to keep up with his stride. "I have learned a lot about them." I tugged at his arm. "That reminds me. I did a nasal inspection, and there was an inordinate amount of pine on Mason's clothes."

Briggs surveyed the ground. "Makes sense if he was dragged across pine needles."

"It does but just as a side note, I smelled an unusual concentration of pine on Ivy Eagleton when I was delivering the brownies to the picnic."

His puzzled expression was always adorable. "You were baking brownies for the bird watching club?" he asked.

"Not me. As you know, my brownies come from a box. They were Elsie's brownies."

He gave his head a short shake. "You're giving me whiplash, Lacey. Let's keep to the part about the pine scent on Ivy."

"You were the one who asked about the brownies," I reminded him. "Anyhow, at the time, I asked Ivy about the pine. She was shocked I could smell it, so I told her about my—" I tapped my nose but put a pause on that part of the conversation because apparently I was giving him *whiplash*. (Insert mental eye roll here.) "Ivy said she'd been perched in a pine tree. She's a photographer more than she's a bird watcher. She said she gets the best shots from a tree branch."

"Makes sense but I'll talk to her." Briggs continued toward the man, John Jacobs, presumably. He was visibly shaken as we reached him.

Briggs showed the man his badge. "I'm Detective Briggs. Were you a friend of Mason Fanning?"

The man nodded and took a visible, deep swallow before speaking. "Can't believe it." His voice was dry and hoarse. He cleared his throat. "I'm sorry. I'm just so shaken up about it."

"And you're—?" Briggs asked.

"Sorry, yes, I'm John Jacobs. I was Mason's friend. I hate to admit, I was probably his only friend."

Briggs flicked a look my way. I had to work not to flash back a cocky smile. So far I'd been right about everything. I only wished I had more insight into who hated Mason the most.

"Is it true someone killed him? He didn't just fall or hurt himself? I can't believe someone from the club would do this," John said.

John smoothed his already slick hair back over his head. My guess would have been that he spent a great deal of time in front of a mirror. He wore a great deal of aftershave too, something with musk, according to my nose. It was definitely a fragrance I would have noticed on Mason's clothing if he had struggled with his attacker and his attacker happened to be his one friend, John Jacobs. That scientific fact and John's genuine reaction to seeing his friend dead was enough to convince me he was not the culprit. Unless, of course, he had killed Mason before rushing back to his home or hotel to freshen up and splash on aftershave so he could put on a great performance of looking utterly shocked. My intuition was not giving that theory a green light. Too far-fetched.

Briggs took his time and let John collect himself again before prodding further.

"Would you say Mason had a lot of enemies?"

John seemed torn on whether to answer. Either he didn't want to get any of his club mates in trouble or he didn't want to talk badly about his dead friend. "Look," he finally said after a long pause, "Mason was sort of an arrogant, cold individual. I'll be the first to admit he took way too much pleasure in other people's pain. There was an incident last night at the convention—" he started.

"With Nora Banks?" Briggs asked.

John looked rightly impressed. "Oh, you've already heard about it."

Briggs cast me a secret wink. "Yes, I understand Mason humiliated Miss Banks in front of the club members."

John nodded sadly. "He did. It was terribly cruel but typical Mason Fanning behavior."

"It makes me curious," Briggs started. I pepped right up wondering if my brilliant boyfriend had already formulated a possibly theory that John was the killer. I waited for the zinger that might very well end the case before it really got started.

(Which would have been thoroughly disappointing.) "Why were you his friend?"

It was a somewhat disappointing end to an intriguing start, but it was a logical question.

John glanced back at Mason's body, then turned back to us. "As hard edged as he was, Mason was an interesting guy. He had several degrees, one in ornithology and one in geology. He knew a lot. We didn't hang out much, but whenever the Society got together for outings and travel trips, I partnered with Mason. He was a competent and knowledgeable bird watching friend." It was a genuine and plausible answer.

One of the Mayfield officers emerged on the trail. "Detective Briggs, the coroner has arrived."

"Thanks, Officer Rowley, show him to the site, please." Briggs turned back to John. "Will you be around? I might have some more questions for you."

John nodded. "Sure, whatever you need."

"By the way, Mr. Jacobs, do you know who we should call? Next of kin?" Briggs asked.

"I think he has a sister. She lives in Australia. I probably have her name somewhere. I'll look for it. Otherwise, Mason was pretty much a loner."

Briggs nodded. "Again, thanks for your help."

CHAPTER 16

*N*ate Blankenship, the local coroner, confirmed that Mason died from a knife wound to the chest. He also confirmed that he didn't die in the shrub but rather was dragged there by his assailant.

Briggs was writing down some of what Nate had confirmed. I pulled out my phone to let Amelia know what was happening. I'd already sent one text letting her know I wouldn't be back right away. She assured me things were under control and that business had slowed since morning.

"I hate to leave," I told Briggs as he finished in his notebook. "You know how I love a good murder," I said quietly so no one else could hear.

"My ghoulish girlfriend." He discretely brushed his hand against mine. "Don't you have a flower shop to run?"

"Detective Briggs," an officer called from an overgrown area fifty feet off the trail. "We've found something." This particular murder scene was taking much longer than the usual scene. The crime had taken place in a thickly forested area, and while the killer had failed at hiding the main piece of evidence, namely the body, they had thus far succeeded at hiding other smaller pieces of evidence, like the murder weapon.

"Oh that's it," I said, "I'm texting Amelia to let her know I'll be delayed. Otherwise, curiosity will eat at me and regret will overwhelm me."

Briggs' tilted grin appeared.

"All right, that might be overdramatic."

I followed close at his heels. "But I still want to see what they found."

Officer Rowley, a young officer with red razor rash on his chin, waved us to a section that was surrounded by the haphazard limbs of trees growing nearby. Briggs lifted a particularly long and dangly one and held it up so I could walk beneath it.

"Right here," Rowley said pointing down to a dark green backpack. It was one of the fancy ones I'd seen at the convention that allowed for your personal belongings and also provided a large pouch for a camera or binoculars. The camera pouch on the backpack was noticeably empty. "Some of the contents are here." He pointed next to the backpack. A notebook with the cover ripped and bent sat next to a tube of suntan lotion and a baggie filled with some sort of trail mix.

Briggs pulled on his gloves and gently moved the backpack back and forth. The top zipper was open. He pulled free a sweatshirt, a folded up plastic rain slicker and a pocket sized guide to North American birds. "Unless the murder was a botched robbery, it seems someone rummaged through the backpack looking for something." He lifted the backpack out of the leafy litter, unzipped the front pocket and pulled out a leather wallet. "If it was a thief, they missed the most prized item."

"Since they didn't even bother with the small zipper, we can probably assume they were looking for something bigger. It seems there are three items missing that would be expected in a bird watcher's backpack," I continued. "Binoculars, a camera and a phone."

Briggs nodded. "And we've already found his binoculars."

"Maybe he wasn't carrying a phone," Rowley offered with a shrug. "My aunt is a big bird watcher. She took me with her to the Rocky Mountains once. My phone went off just as we were closing in on some kind of jay, can't remember the species. My phone sent it off into the trees. She was so mad," Rowley said. "Maybe he wasn't carrying a phone because he didn't want to scare off the birds."

"Well, phones have this magical little setting that allows you to put them on silent," Briggs said. There was a touch of sarcasm in the tone, but I knew he was going easy on the guy. He was young, a rookie probably.

Rowley chuckled. "Guess that's why you're the detective. So do you want me to get a large evidence bag?" He really was a rookie.

Briggs looked up at him. "That's probably a good idea. And, Rowley, while you're walking that direction, look to see if John Jacobs, the victim's friend is still hanging around the picnic area. He's wearing a light green polo shirt and gray pants. Walk him this way when you return."

A text came through on my phone. It was Amelia's reply. "No problem. Things are fine here." I read. "Guess that means I can stick around for awhile. Why are you bringing John here?"

Briggs put the backpack down. "Well, fellow investigator, you tell me." There was a teasing lilt to his tone, but he was genuinely interested to see if I could figure out his reasoning.

I tapped my chin and gazed down at the backpack and the tossed out contents. "Ah ha, I've got it. You're hoping since John was Mason's friend, he'll be able to tell you exactly what is missing from the backpack."

Briggs nodded appreciatively. "Well done. Hopefully John

knows enough about his buddy to let us know what's missing and possibly even why it might be missing."

Officer Rowley returned quickly and efficiently, just like a rookie trying his hardest to do things right. John Jacobs returned with him, a questioning expression on his face.

"Detective Briggs," John said as he followed Rowley around the maze of shrubs and dangling tree limbs. "You wanted to see me?" he asked just as he reached the small clearing where we stood. His gaze dropped instantly to the backpack. "That's Mason's pack. I wondered where that went. He never goes out bird watching without it." He looked up at Briggs. "It looks as if someone has rifled through it. He would never leave the zipper open."

"Yes, we found it like that," Briggs explained as he pulled out a pair of gloves for John. "I was hoping you could look at all the items I've pulled out and the several items that were strewn about when the assailant went though Mason's things. It would be helpful if you could tell us what is missing from his usual gear. Not including the binoculars that you already identified as belonging to the victim."

John's head bobbed in quick, short nods. "Yes, yes of course. Anything I can do to help." He pulled on the gloves and pinched the rain slicker and sweatshirt between two fingers, apparently worried he'd damage evidence if he handled the things too roughly. He took his task quite seriously and took note of the items already on the ground, including the wallet. Then he lifted the backpack and spun it around to the camera pouch. He looked back at the items on the ground and turned to Briggs. "Where's the camera? Mason never went into the wilderness without his camera." He looked into the now emptied bag. "His phone is gone too. We always take our phones for safety reasons and for the occasional spontaneous photo. Sometimes the camera isn't practical. But Mason would never walk out here without those two tools."

Briggs pulled out his notebook. "Do you happen to know what kind of camera he carried?"

"Sure, it was a Canon EOS."

"This question will be harder," Briggs warned. "Do you know why someone would want it? Was it especially valuable?"

John considered the question. "It wasn't a particularly valuable camera." He snapped his fingers. "Wait." He tapped the side of his head. "I don't know why this didn't come to me sooner. Late last night, after the convention had closed for the night, Mason met me in the hotel bar for a beer. He told me he had taken a very important picture. He said it was rare, and it would have significant consequences."

Briggs and I snapped to full attention. "Did he tell you the contents of the photo or why it would be significant?" Briggs asked.

"No, he didn't give out any details but told me I'd see it soon. I just assumed it was a photo of a rare bird. Three years ago, Mason won a prestigious award for a photo of a California condor feeding its chick. It was a spectacular shot. I'm not sure what he had this time, but it sounded important."

"Important enough for someone to steal the camera?" Briggs asked.

"And possibly the phone for the same reason," I added. Both men looked at me. "Did he tell you if he caught this photo on his camera or phone?"

John rubbed his chin. "No, come to think of it he didn't say. I guess I just assumed it would be the camera but you're perfectly right. I've known fellow bird watchers to catch a spontaneous and terrific photo on a camera phone. Like I said, sometimes it's inconvenient to pull out a camera." He chuckled lightly. "Most birds don't wait around for the pose."

"No?" Briggs glanced my direction. "I know of at least one who would." He brushed past the comment that was meant only for me.

"Thank you for your help with this, Mr. Jacobs. We're going to collect up Mr. Fanning's things for evidence."

"I sure hope you find who did this," John said. "Mason wasn't exactly citizen of the year, but he didn't deserve this."

Briggs nodded in agreement. "We'll catch the killer soon."

John hiked his way back out of the clearing and headed along the trail.

"So, Detective Briggs, do you think the motive had something to do with the mystery photo?" I asked.

"Seems like it might be a clue." Rowley took care of the evidence collection, and Briggs and I headed out of the clearing.

I sighed. "Guess I need to get back to my place of business."

"Detective Briggs," an officer called as we reached the trail. "We've found the weapon."

I shrugged. "Or maybe I could stick it out for a few more minutes."

CHAPTER 17

$\mathcal{B}$riggs and I met up with the police officers who had found what was presumed to be the murder weapon. The blood smear on the six inch blade made it fairly certain. The pearl handled knife with its high carbon steel blade was nestled in a thick layer of loamy soil behind a large boulder. Oddly enough, the killer had taken the time and energy to attempt the impossible task of hiding the body, but they hardly bothered to hide the small knife. It was found only three hundred yards from the tree where Mason was murdered, and while the blade was slightly hidden by the soil, the white pearl handle could hardly be missed. There were infinite locations one could hide a six inch knife in a dense forest, but the killer merely jammed the blade into the earth and left it virtually in the open for the police to find.

Briggs had the same thought. (It was part of the reason we were so perfectly matched.) "Interesting. It seems almost as if the killer was hoping we'd find the weapon."

"You took the words right out of my mouth," I said. "It would have been easy to hide that knife anywhere in this forest where it would have taken days to find." I looked at Briggs. "I'll bet you a dinner out that there aren't any prints on that pearl handle."

"That would be a fool's bet, but I'll take you to dinner win or lose." Briggs pulled out his phone and took a few pictures of the position and area around the knife. "Evidence bag, please" Briggs said as he stuck out a gloved hand. "I'm going to show it to the club members. Maybe someone can point us in the direction of the owner." He stooped down with the bag and carefully pinched the handle so as not so smear any prints that might be there. The blood was dry and the knife went cleanly into the bag. "Good work, officers. Keep looking. We're missing a camera and a phone."

The two officers got right back to their search. I followed Briggs back toward the picnic area. Nate and his team had placed Mason's body in the bag. They were getting ready to transport him to the morgue. They would have no choice but to roll the gurney with the macabre body bag past the stunned club members.

"Let's hurry. I want to see the reactions of the others as Nate rolls the body to the van," Briggs said.

"Something tells me there won't be torrents of tears and wet tissues," I added.

We hiked along the path and headed toward the voices rolling up from the picnic area. The club members had gathered at various tables. Nora was still noticeably absent. The murder hadn't stopped them from enjoying Elsie's irresistible brownies. The tables were strewn with empty plates dotted with a few fudgy crumbs. And only a few, Elsie's brownies almost always prompted finger dabbing to get every last morsel. Nate's gurney wheels squeaked causing a few faces to fade white. Everyone pushed up from the picnic benches, and hats were pulled off in respect. But as I predicted, no tears or tissues.

Briggs, also out of respect, waited for Nate's team to load the body into the coroner's van and pull out of the parking lot before approaching Mason's fellow club members with the key piece of evidence.

Andrew spotted us walking toward the picnic area. He'd snapped out of his stupor and taken charge, it seemed. "Detective Briggs, we're getting tired. We'd like to head back to our hotel rooms. It's been a trying day." His eyes swept down to the evidence bag in Briggs' hand. "Nora's knife." He took a dramatic short breath. "Why are you holding Nora's knife?" His deep set eyes swept the area and his dark brows furrowed. "Where is Nora? Come to think of it, I haven't seen her since the beginning of the picnic." His exceptionally baritone voice rolled easily to his friends. Instantly, whispers and shocked gasps mingled with the usual bird twitters and rhythmic tune of waves curling and splashing along the coastline.

Briggs kept it straight and professional. Setting off a hurricane of rumors and accusations was not going to help the case. "Can you confirm that this knife belongs to Nora Banks?"

A few more club members, including Minnie, the treasurer, moved cautiously toward Briggs and his seemingly damning bag of evidence. "Oh my." Minnie pressed her hand against the colorful silk scarf that was draped haphazardly yet fashionably around her neck.

Andrew swept his fingers anxiously across one thick brow. "Minnie, this looks like Nora's knife, doesn't it? I certainly don't want to confirm it without the rest of you agreeing." He glanced at the other stricken faces (some still wearing tiny bits of Elsie's brownies on their shirts and at the edges of their mouths). Heads nodded, reluctantly. It seemed no one was keen to implicate one of their own in a heinous crime.

Minnie took a deep breath. "Nora's father gave it to her last Christmas. She kept it in a leather pouch on the side of her back-pack. It was for protection, in case she found herself deep in the forest or desert or some other rugged place where a knife would come in handy." Minnie's face brightened. "Almost all of us have them." Her moment of positive enthusiasm dimmed. "But I'm sure that one belongs to Nora."

Ivy had joined the group. "It's a particularly pretty one with the mother of pearl handle and all." Ivy peered up from the bag in Briggs' hand. "Is that how Mason died? We've heard little, so far."

"It would be nice to know if we need to take our own precautions," an older man with a rust colored mustache and a t-shirt that proclaimed 'easily distracted by birds' said sharply.

Briggs lowered the bag to pull it out of the center of attention. It seemed to be making everyone uncomfortable. Uneasy feet shuffles and supportive pats on the back made their way around the semi circle of people who had joined us.

"We found this near the victim," Briggs said solemnly, "but we have no proof yet that this knife was used in Mason Fanning's murder."

Just hearing the word murder caused vibrations through the group.

"So there is a murderer somewhere out here," a woman said as she crossed her arms defensively. She followed the protective move with a shifty eyed glance around the half circle.

"Nora had good reason to hate Mason," the mustache man said. "He humiliated her in front of everyone last night."

Andrew, who thus far had seemed amiable enough but had shown little inclination to take charge as club president, finally found his leadership voice. He cleared his throat. "Everyone, let's not panic or jump to conclusions. Admittedly, this is frightening, but let's not jump to conclusions or fall right into the trap of unbridled fear. I'm sure Detective Briggs will use the evidence gathered"— Andrew looked pointedly at the evidence bag and the pearl handled knife—"to find the killer. In the meantime, we must keep it together."

Briggs nodded his appreciation to Andrew. "Do any of you

know where I can find Nora Banks? Any idea at all where she might be?"

There was a silent pause, but this time it didn't seem to stem from people trying to avoid implicating a friend. They seemed genuinely perplexed.

"I know she said she was going to go on her own birding adventure." Ivy looked at me. "Remember, I told you she ate a sandwich and then left the picnic."

"Yes, I remember," I said. "Did anyone happen to hear her plans? Did she tell anyone where she was going?"

A chorus of no's and head shakes followed.

"That's breaking one of our most prominent rules," Andrew added with a scowl. "We always tell at least one club member where we're going when we head off on our own. Apparently, she was still too upset about last night."

"Either that or she didn't want anyone to know where she was because—" Minnie's words trailed off. "No, that can't be. It just doesn't seem possible that Nora could be responsible."

Briggs seemed to decide that was a good point to end the conversation. People were growing agitated. With that type of stress, people tended to jump to wild rumors and theories. Although, admittedly, theorizing that Nora might have murdered Mason wasn't all that wild.

"Thank you all for your time. My officers will probably take down personal information, phone numbers and where you're staying. Please cooperate. That way we can reach you if we need to. While it never hurts to be cautious, try not to worry too much. We'll find the person soon enough."

Briggs and I walked away. I was just about to ask how he felt about the whole discussion and whether or not he got any inkling about what happened to Mason when my phone buzzed. It was a text from Amelia.

"You should probably return to the shop." It was all she wrote, but it was easy enough to read the urgency in her words.

"I've got to head back to the flower shop." I smiled at him. "Do you think you can handle things without me for a bit?"

He glanced around, took hold of my hand and brought it to his mouth for a discrete kiss. "I'll try to manage."

CHAPTER 18

By the time I reached the store, the scene inside seemed quite normal. Barbara was finishing up with a customer and Amelia was on the phone, with a customer, I presumed since she was using her professional voice, a soft, overly polite without being condescending tone that she told me she'd formulated during her job as a hostess at a large, posh restaurant. There was nothing amiss on the crow side of the shop either. My bird had tucked his beak under for a brief nap in the late afternoon sun coming through the shop window. Apparently, I'd misread Amelia's text.

Amelia hung up with the customer and tugged at the slight curl in her tawny brown hair as she cast me a look that made it seem that the normal, placid scene in the shop was not what it seemed.

Barbara smiled brightly at the woman she was helping as she handed her a mixed bouquet of pink roses and white carnations. "Here you go, Mrs. Shuster. I'm so glad you decided to take my suggestion and go with the pink rather than the yellow roses."

Mrs. Shuster, a woman who was an occasional customer, didn't look altogether convinced about the pink roses. She stared at them in the way my ten-year-old self used to stare at the broccoli on my plate. "It's just that yellow roses are my aunt's favorites," she said meekly. I hadn't known her to be a shy or particularly reserved woman, but it seemed she'd been almost berated into accepting that the pink roses were better. I shot a glance toward Amelia. She nodded slightly and then tugged at the curl in her hair. It was a gesture I'd never seen her do before.

I cleared my throat, catching the customer's attention for the first time.

"Oh, Lacey," Mrs. Shuster said with relief. "I didn't see you come in." She looked askance at Barbara before favoring me with a weak smile.

It was time to hop into action. "Mrs. Shuster, if you prefer to have the yellow roses, then we'd be happy to replace the pink with yellow. We'll add in a few extra for free for the inconvenience."

Mrs. Shuster's face lit up. "Would you? That would be so nice." She turned a gracious smile toward Barbara, who looked as if she had just removed a tart lemon from her mouth.

"As I explained to Mrs. Shuster," Barbara pushed herself right into the conversation, "the pink roses are a much nicer contrast to the white carnations."

Mrs. Shuster's earlier, hopeful posture deflated again.

"I think the yellow roses will contrast just fine," I said curtly. "I'll tell you what, Mrs. Shuster. I'll make the new arrangement myself. Barbara," I said forcing a polite tone, "there are three bouquets in the freezer that need to be delivered before the end of the work day. The recipients are all in the same few mile radius in Mayfield. I'll pay you extra for mileage, of course, but it would be a great help to me if you could deliver them."

For the first time since she'd walked into my shop, Barbara seemed to be speechless. She was also reluctant to leave the task of making a new arrangement to me. It was going to take all my strength to keep her on. If only she weren't so good at her job. Elsie was right. Why did all the good ones have to come with hard to overlook flaws?

"Yes, I'll deliver them," Barbara finally said. "I'll make note of my mileage for the reimbursement."

"Perfect." I turned back to Mrs. Shuster and took the pink bouquet from her hands. "Let's get you those yellow roses."

Barbara hurried off to the refrigerator. She kept a watchful eye on my bouquet building as she carried the three deliveries to her car. I half expected her to stop and move a rose or carnation to what she considered a more appropriate place, only, it seemed, she'd had more than enough of Mrs. Shuster and her yellow roses. Thankfully, she walked out of the shop with her purse and a slight ding to her pride. Obviously, we would need to have a chat about letting the customers choose their own flowers.

A much cheerier Mrs. Shuster walked out with her bright yellow roses. With the shop now clear of customers and Barbara, Amelia dropped right into a long complaint.

Her head was shaking, and she was still fidgeting with her hair. "I just don't think she should have been so pushy with Mrs. Shuster." She tugged at a curl. Her hair came just to her shoulders. Most days, she curled it lightly, so it bounced playfully around her face. (Unlike my un-light curls that bounced like Tigger from the Hundred Acre Wood.)

"I agree. I'll talk to her about it, but I think Mrs. Shuster left happy so disaster averted." I squinted at her as she tussled with another strand of hair. "Amelia, is everything all right? I've never seen you fidget with your hair."

She dropped her arms as if they suddenly weighed fifty pounds. "Am I fidgeting? I didn't realize." Her face dropped and a frown pulled down the corners of her mouth. She released a disconcerted breath as she looked up. "Do you think my hairstyle makes me look too young? Barbara said it reminded her of her twelve-year-old niece. She said I should wear it longer and straighter so I can look my age."

"She's utterly wrong, Amelia." I could feel heat rising in my face. "You have to ignore her. She has been changing all of my bouquets, making me feel as if I don't know what I'm doing. I started to question my skills, but now I know Barbara is just one of those people who has to control every situation."

Amelia looked happier. "A control freak. That's what my mom calls my Aunt Gigi. Whenever my mom does the holiday meal, Aunt Gigi comes in and tries to change things. She'll even sneak extra seasoning into my mom's gravy, and it's the best tasting gravy in the world." She breathed in and out. "I feel so much better just talking to you. I was feeling so self-conscious about what she said and then poor Mrs. Shuster came in and Barbara turned her control freakiness on her. As much as Mrs. Shuster begged for yellow roses, Barbara just wasn't going to let her walk out with yellow. I'm so glad you came back in time to give her the flowers she wanted."

"Me too and Barbara and I will definitely be having a chat about all of this."

Amelia's face smoothed like marble. "No, please don't bring up the hair thing. I don't want her to think she got to me."

"You're right. I'll only talk to her about the yellow roses. She's going to have to change her behavior, or she's just not going to work out."

Amelia set to work cleaning up after Mrs. Shuster's bouquet. "I know how badly you need her. I only wish I had an ounce of talent with flowers."

"You have other talents that are much more valuable. Thank you for keeping the shop running smoothly. I'm sorry I was out so long. There was an incident when I delivered the brownies."

She looked up with big brown eyes. "I heard someone died. A friend of mine texted that the coroner's van was at Mayfield Park." She lifted her shoulders coyly. "Was your cute boyfriend at the scene?"

"He was. I occasionally help out on a case." I tapped my nose. "My super sniffer notices things that the police can't smell."

Comprehension washed over her. "That makes sense. What a great tool for them to have. A super sniffer. Was it murder?"

I didn't normally broadcast murders, but she'd been kind enough to watch over the shop and endure Barbara's ridiculous criticism so she deserved to know. "Yes, it seems that way." Bringing the case back up reminded me that Nora Banks had spent some birding time at the lighthouse. It was possible she'd returned. "In fact, since we've slowed down for the day, and since Miss Opinion-ator is out on deliveries, would you mind terribly if I took a quick jaunt down to the beach? I think I might find someone who knew the victim down there. She likes to watch for birds by the lighthouse."

"Sure thing." Amelia picked up the last few leaves and stems. "Don't worry about a thing. Kingston and I will handle it." She stopped her task for a second. "What should I say if she brings up my hair again? I badly wanted to mention that tight bun she wears. It reminds me of my kindergarten teacher, and she was like a hundred and fifty years old. But then I didn't want to be mean like Barbara."

"Good for you, Amelia." I walked over and gave her a quick squeeze. "We both have to stay strong. When she's getting to us, we'll just give each other this wink." I demonstrated. "That helps remind us that she can't help it. She just has to control things like your Aunt Gigi. That doesn't mean we have to listen to her advice. We can just humor her and let her think she's in charge."

Amelia squeezed me back. "Thanks, Lacey. This really helped. I was about to go home and toss out my curling iron." She leaned back and we practiced the wink. "Go on your walk. Good luck finding the person you're looking for."

"Thanks and text if you need me. I'll just be a ten minute dash away."

CHAPTER 19

A hearty sun had left behind enough heat between the blue
sky and the cement sidewalk that each step produced a
cradle of warm air around my feet and legs. Daylight was starting
to make its slow, glorious descent into late afternoon, and sparkles
of light flickered off the choppy edges of water along the coast.
The late day off-shore breeze had churned the ocean into its usual
uneasy dance of sharp, quick interval waves. A brave sailboat
traversed the rough surface as it torpedoed with full fat sails along
the coast.

I picked up my pace and crossed my fingers that some of the
fall prone Shearwaters that Nora was hoping for had made their
unusual summer debut. I was allowing myself the very real possibility that even if Nora had ventured out to the lighthouse, she
would no longer be there. Certainly, word would have reached her
that Mason Fanning was dead. It seemed her birding peers would
also have informed her about the knife being found. More than
once, I considered the possibility that if I did meet up with her, I
might be facing a killer, one who knew she was going to be

arrested for murder. It wouldn't be the first time I'd found myself in that unfortunate predicament, and it generally earned me a lecture about the dangers of approaching a suspect. And yet, I'd once again found myself in the same situation. I blamed my insatiable appetite for solving a murder. If I could get to a possible suspect before the police that was like frosting on a delicious cupcake. Besides, Nora was petite and not terribly menacing in demeanor or size. How dangerous could she be (especially without her pearl handled knife)?

I took a short jaunt along the wharf to the steps leading down to the ivory sand. It was late enough that most beachgoers had already packed up their umbrellas and ice chests for the day, but a group of determined teenagers were attempting a game of volleyball. The afternoon breeze was not helping. Aside from a couple walking along the shore and another small group huddled on towels eating hot dogs, the sand was empty. No sign of a bird watcher.

I shaded my eyes and glanced along the coast to the lighthouse. Nora was sitting on a smooth rock with her knees bent, holding her legs. Her chin was resting on the tops of her knees. She looked more like a little girl waiting for her turn at jump rope than a woman searching for rare birds.

I hurried off the beach, over the wharf and across to the lighthouse. I followed the narrow hiking path that snaked down to the beach and rocks below the lighthouse.

The constant roar of the ocean muted my approach. Nora was rightly startled by my sudden appearance a few rocks away. She put her hands down to steady herself and keep from slipping along the smooth rock. Her backpack sat next to her, loaded down with all her birding tools. I sensed instantly from the drawn look on her face that she'd heard the news. I wondered if she was worried this was about to come down around her.

I approached with caution, but she still pushed abruptly to her feet as if a shark had just climbed up on the rocks to eat her. I put up my hands.

"Don't worry, I'm just here to make sure you're all right. I saw you from the beach and you looked upset." It was a flimsy excuse, and she wasn't buying it.

Her drawn face took on more of a puzzled scowl. "I don't understand." She glanced at the beach and then back at me. "How did you see me? How could you tell I was upset? Were you looking for me?" She leaned slightly to the right and looked past me, expectantly.

"I'm alone," I said and then wondered if that was the smartest thing to admit. Still, even though she was suddenly on edge, I just didn't feel any sense of danger. My adrenaline was always pretty reliable and kicked into action when needed. It was staying out of the mix . . . for now. That realization prompted me to be more honest with Nora.

I took a couple steps closer, but we were still a few good slabs of rock apart. She didn't back up, so I took it as my opening.

"Nora, I assume you heard about Mason."

Again, she looked perplexed. "I don't understand. How did you know that? Aren't you a florist?" There was just enough conde-scension in her tone to sting but I forged ahead. After all, the woman was probably going to be arrested for murder. I could overlook a little patronization.

"I was at the club picnic when they discovered Mason's body. I had delivered the brownies Andrew ordered from my friend's bakery."

The wind had left her cheeks bright red. It seemed she'd been sitting out on the rocks all afternoon. If she had, then she certainly couldn't have killed Mason. Even if she had come back to the rocks to hide, why wouldn't she have left town?

"Minnie, the club treasurer, texted me the news." Nora looked frail as she crossed her arms around herself. "She just sent me another text that they found my knife near the body." She hugged herself tighter. The color drained from her face. "I think I might throw up." She dropped to her knees on the rocks and leaned over for a few minutes before sitting back on her heels and taking deep swallows of air.

"Can I get you anything? Some water?" I offered, although it was not exactly convenient considering where we were standing.

A larger than normal wave smacked the rocks below hard enough to send a cool salty mist our way. It seemed to revive Nora. She pushed to her feet.

"I have no idea how my knife got there." She waved her hand toward her backpack. "It's usually sheathed right there in the leather pouch on the side of my pack. My father gave it to me and I cherish it." She laughed silently but enough to shake her shoulders. "The only thing I've ever used it for was to cut open a package of beef jerky and to pry open a can of beans when I forgot my can opener. I certainly would never use it to kill anyone." Another laugh. "I would never use anything to kill someone. I was angry with Mason. I probably hated him more than I've ever hated anyone, but I would never kill him."

Nora leaned over and pulled her phone out of the front pocket on her backpack. "I haven't texted anyone back. I've just been sitting here trying to absorb the information. I always do my best thinking when I'm in nature."

"I think most of us do our best thinking like that. But you should consider heading into town before rumors get out of hand. You need to tell the police what you just told me."

Her face jerked my direction. "The police? Are they looking for me? I knew I would be blamed for this. Everyone saw what happened last night." Her eyes grew wider. "You witnessed me this morning threatening Mason. They were just idle threats," she said urgently.

"I know they were. I'll be sure to let the police know that you calmed down immediately after—if they ask, that is. I'm not even sure it'll come to that. Were you here, on these rocks, all afternoon?"

"Yes, yes I was here." She held out her red arms. "Apparently, I didn't put on enough sunblock."

"Normally, I would say that's a big no-no. This time it might help your alibi. What about other people or friends who might have seen you out here? People who can vouch for your whereabouts."

Nora stared down toward the ocean for a moment, then her shoulders drooped. "I haven't talked to anyone. There were a few kids climbing the rocks at one point, and a couple who came halfway down the trail to take selfies but that's all. I had my phone on silent, something I usually do when I'm watching for birds. I didn't notice Minnie's text for a good hour. The second one about the knife came a half hour later. I wasn't sure what to do. I'm scared they'll blame me."

"You just need to explain everything to the police. It'll be fine but you should probably do that soon. The longer you stay out here, the more it'll look as if you're hiding something."

Her face flattened, and the red in her cheeks erased. "I hadn't thought of that. You're right." She leaned over and picked up her backpack for the trek back across the rocks. It was a solidly filled satchel, reminding me of my high school backpack when it was filled with textbooks.

It took petite Nora a good amount of effort to lift the bag onto her shoulders and then hike across the slippery rocks with the heavy load on her back. It sure would have been a nearly impossible feat for someone Nora's size to drag a large body across the forest floor. I kept that little detail tucked in my brain for another time. For now, Nora needed to go to the police. My intuition told me she was telling the truth, but it was always possible (however unlikely) that, in this particular case, my intuition was wrong. Either way, she needed to talk to Briggs and the sooner the better.

CHAPTER 20

*B*arbara returned from her delivery errand just seconds after I got back to the shop. Amelia's face soured the moment Barbara walked through the door. Naturally, Barbara went into a long opinion about how deliveries would be easier if she had the right kind of boxes or baskets to put in the backseat of her car. On this point, she was probably more correct than needlessly bossy.

I had no sooner sat at my computer to finish paperwork for the day when the shop bell rang and Elsie's familiar 'I have treats' hummed down the hallway. The trip to the beach had given me a renewed appetite for one of her goodies. I took a deep whiff before I reached the front of the shop. It was a little game I liked to play where I tried to guess what yummy thing would be waiting for me out front. My nose was telling me something with rum.

"Ho, ho, ho and a bottle of rum," I chortled as I walked to the front of the shop. Much to Elsie's chagrin, Barbara was already pushing a dark cocoa covered rum ball into her mouth. Fortunately, Elsie had brought more than one. (Otherwise, it might have been grounds for dismissal.)

"That nose of yours." Elsie shook her head. "These are rum balls I made from that seven layer wedding cake where the groom got cold feet at the rehearsal dinner. Since it was paid for, I tried to get them to take it, but the bride said it was too heartbreaking to look at. So . . ." She waved at the plate full of cocoa coated chocolate balls. "The most expensive rum balls you'll ever taste."

The rich chocolaty and rum-y smell drew me directly to the plate. I didn't hesitate to push a rich, fudgy bauble between my lips. "Hmm," I said as I waved Amelia over to try one. While Barbara had helped herself, polite Amelia had waited to be invited for a taste. "I haven't had a rum ball in a long time, Elsie. These are perfect. Just the right amount of rum."

"Although," Barbara piped up as she helped herself to a second one. I held my breath waiting to see if she was actually going to have the nerve to criticize one of Elsie's baked goods. Elsie's nostrils flared in anticipation too. "Some crushed walnuts would help to break up the sweetness."

I was still holding the breath as I braved a glance toward Elsie. I hardly needed to look her direction. I could already feel the tension rolling off my friend in waves. Elsie rarely deserved any kind of criticism, particularly when it came to her baked goods. In general, about the only thing I could find to criticize Elsie about was the fact that she didn't take criticism well.

"Well, next time *you* make rum balls, you can add walnuts," Elsie said sharply.

Barbara, who apparently after years of offering up advice and criticism had grown numb to sarcasm and harsh retorts, went right on with her unwanted opinion. "Walnuts, in general, are an excellent addition to baked goods. Just this morning, I was enjoying one of your cinnamon croissants, and I kept thinking how much better it would be with some finely chopped walnuts."

Amelia had scampered off to the potting sink. I wanted to

follow her but decided I needed to stick around to clean up the pieces after Elsie's head exploded. Fortunately, clean up was not needed.

Elsie fluttered an annoyed blink my direction and effectively turned so she was facing away from Barbara. She rolled her eyes and took a deep breath before spinning on her heels and heading toward the door.

"Thanks for the treats," I called to her before the door shut. She didn't look back. I'd have to send her a text to apologize. I took my own deep breath and turned to Barbara. She was completely oblivious to how rude she'd been. She really was an odd bird. It seemed it was time for our chat.

"Barbara," I started.

She sucked in a loud gasp. "Oh my, I forgot to tell you what I heard when I was out on delivery." It seemed I wasn't going to get my two cents in quite yet. Barbara's perfectly drawn in brows danced up and down. "Apparently, there was a terrible murder in Mayfield. A man was shot dead right in the wilderness area of the park. It was some sort of squabble"—she waved a hand—"Most likely a lover's quarrel. Crimes of passion always lead to someone dying." She spoke with all the confidence and authority of an expert. "It was quite the horror scene, blood everywhere," she added in between short sips of breath. "They've already made the arrest." Since almost everything she claimed was flatly wrong, I didn't startle too much at her last proclamation. It was the only part I was interested in.

"They've made an arrest?" I asked warily. "Where did you hear that?"

"Well, I stopped at the gas station on the way out of town, you know the one with the Grab 'N' Go Mart. There was a woman at the next pump. She told me all about the murder and the arrest. The scorned lover, naturally. Some women just don't know how to deal with men." It seemed Barbara was also an expert on relationships, even though I'd garnered from our short chats while arranging flowers that she had no one in particular in her life. Still, it made me wonder whether I'd been wrong about Nora. (Although, she was absolutely not Mason's lover.) But what if she'd walked into the police station and confessed to the whole thing? Or had the knife been enough evidence for an arrest? I was going to have to text Briggs, but first I needed a chat with Barbara. Only that was harder than I expected.

"Barbara," I started again in a firm tone.

"What should I do next? I was thinking I might rearrange the cooler before closing. It's a little cluttered and chaotic."

I sighed silently. (There was a slight groan too.) "I prefer the cooler to stay exactly the same. It's the way Ryder and I have arranged it and it works." It was the first time I'd mentioned Ryder, the person she was temporarily replacing. It seemed I was starting to miss him a lot. But was he actually going to want to return to this quaint, mundane job after months in the Amazon? Gosh, I sure hoped so.

Barbara didn't seem capable of hearing the word no. Maybe she had somehow managed to block it from her brain, or perhaps, she just couldn't process the notion that someone would turn down her idea. Her drawn in brows, brows that were starting to seem more ridiculous with each moment, arched and nearly touched before relaxing. "I'll just make a few changes." With that she whisked off to the cooler.

I stood tongue-tied and feeling like a complete bonehead. I glanced across at Amelia. She was staying focused on cleaning the potting table while working her hardest not to make eye contact with me. She'd obviously heard the entire exchange.

"She's exhausting," I muttered. Amelia chuckled to herself as she wiped the table.

I pulled out my phone and sent Briggs a text. "Did you talk to Nora Banks?"

He rang back.

My smile was instant. "Hello, Detective Briggs."

"Hello, Miss Pinkerton. Yes, Nora Banks told me the nice florist in town told her she should go to the police station and talk to Detective Briggs." There was just a hint of annoyance in his tone. "Which means you decided to approach a possible suspect on your own."

"Yes but this particular suspect was not the least bit scary or dangerous. And I knew she wasn't armed because you had her knife in evidence."

"Lacey," he started.

"Yes, I know what you're going to say. But let's get to the important part. Did you talk to her?"

He decided to drop the subsequent lecture. "She came in and told me about her missing knife and that she'd spent the day at the lighthouse watching for birds. Her sunburn sort of confirmed that. However, she also admitted that she despised Mason, and she told me about what he'd done the night before and her threats the next day in front of Les's shop."

"Sounds like she really came clean then. That's good. Are you still considering her a suspect?"

"Unfortunately, a sunburn isn't an ironclad alibi, and she had no one to corroborate that she was at the lighthouse all afternoon. She stays on the list, but I have my doubts."

"She's too small," we said simultaneously. Our laughs were in unison too.

"We are quite the duo," I said. "Great minds think alike."

"Yep and are you thinking Italian for dinner?" he asked. "I'm craving some lasagna."

"Hmm, sounds good. Count me in. Now I've got to go to the

cooler to make sure my new assistant isn't moving everything around so that I can't find anything. See you later."

"I know I'm just wasting my breath, but stay out of danger," he added just before disconnecting the call.

There was a great deal of noise coming from the cooler. I looked at Amelia. She just shrugged in response.

"Ryder, Ryder, Ryder," I muttered as I took a deep breath and headed toward the hallway.

CHAPTER 21

*B*arbara's changes in the cooler were minor enough that I decided not to stress about it. I was, however, relieved when it was time for her to pack up for the day. Amelia normally helped me close up, but since she'd watched over the shop while I was out finding dead bodies and tracking down suspects, I insisted she take off too. There was some selfishness in my gesture. The thought of spending the last thirty minutes of business hours all by myself sounded splendid. Not that Amelia was ever a problem, but alone time was always nice.

I'd sat at my computer to finish some orders while both women collected up their purses and keys from the office. They didn't speak one word to each other. So much for my visions of a cohesive work team. Barbara and her unwanted opinions had caused Amelia to keep her distance. The bell on the door broke the chilly silence in the office.

"I'll get it," Barbara chirped.

"No, I'll get it," Amelia said briskly. "I'm the sales assistant."

"The two of you are on your way out. I'll get it." I pushed up from my desk.

Both women, purses on shoulders, still rushed ahead of me to the front of the shop. I followed behind. "You two have a nice night," I said to let them know I expected them to go home. Unfortunately, the extraordinarily handsome man standing in the shop front caused both women to let the purses slide from their shoulders. Chins dropped for a moment, but Barbara was the first to collect herself. She pushed her purse aside.

"How can I help you?" she asked. There was a tiny sashay in her step as she moved.

"Again, Barbara," Amelia said through slightly gritted teeth. "I'm in charge of helping customers." She pushed her purse aside too and tried to jump in front of Barbara.

Poor Dash glanced helplessly over their heads at me.

I couldn't hold back an amused grin. "Actually, girls, this is my friend. He's just here to chat, so the two of you can go home. See you in the morning."

Profound disappointment crossed their faces, but they both took an extra few seconds to admire the beautiful man before trudging back to their purses.

Amelia was still staring starry eyed at Dash as she sauntered toward the door. "Wait, I've seen you down at the marina," she said. "You work on the boats."

"I find boats so interesting," Barbara said, not to be outdone.

Dash nodded. "Yes, I work on boats, and I find them interesting too."

"See you tomorrow," I said again, with a little more force this time.

They finally walked out, but both stretched up to look through the front window once more.

I couldn't stop a laugh. "Good thing you don't come in here often. To what do I owe this visit?"

Dash was awash in a glowing tan, and the summer sun had

bleached his hair gold. I really couldn't blame Barbara and Amelia. He was always a sight to see.

"Actually, I am here to buy flowers." He headed straight over to pet Kingston on the head.

"And here I thought you just dropped by to visit a friend." I reached into the shelf for Kingston's treat can and carried it over for Dash to give him one.

Dash held a treat out for Kingston's long beak. "You mean the friend I can visit merely by walking out my front door?"

"True. So, who are the flowers for?" I said with a teasing grin. "And if you say for an aunt who just had gallbladder surgery, I'm going to be sorely disappointed."

"Not gallbladder. It was her hip." He patted Kingston once more and turned his own teasing smile (a much more dashing one) on me. "Not true either. I've got a date."

"Oh, do you?" It had been a few weeks since we'd spoken, but the last time we chatted, he was still bringing up his long distance relationship with Elsie's niece, Britney. I waited expectantly for him to fill me in on the details. Not that he was bound to do so, but I would feel terribly disappointed if he didn't.

We headed back to the work counter. "Britney and I have come to a mutual agreement. She's probably going to spend at least another year in Europe, so it just doesn't make sense to keep things going. We've decided to see other people."

"Does Elsie know?" I asked.

Dash shrugged. "Not sure but she'll be glad to hear it." Elsie was never thrilled with their relationship, mostly because Britney obsessed about it and Dash was far too casual about it all. Naturally, as was often the case with men, once Britney was on her way to France to further her culinary career, Dash instantly regretted that he let her go so easily. But it seemed the long distance between them had finally broken the tie for good.

"Is this a rose kind of date?" I had an ulterior motive for asking. I wanted to know more without being too nosy.

He raked his hair back with his fingers. "It's more of a carnation or daisy date. A first date. We met down at the airport. Tiffany is learning to fly planes. She's learning from Bart, the guy who taught me."

"Ah ha, that sounds promising if you both like airplanes. It's always nice to have something in common."

Dash's green eyes sparkled with amusement. "Like solving murder cases?"

"Yes, I suppose that is something James and I have in common." I put up a finger signaling I needed to pause the conversation. I hurried to the cooler. It took me an extra few seconds to find the carnations that Barbara had inexplicably moved to the opposite side. I grabbed a vase of pink and white carnations and a few mauve colored Gerber daisies to add to the mix. It wasn't every day that I got to create an arrangement for Dash.

"Will these do?" I asked as I placed the flowers on the island.

"Sure, those look nice. Don't really know what type of flowers she likes," he admitted.

"I don't think you're required to know that until the third date. Unless your good friend just happens to own a flower shop, then by the second date."

Dash chuckled. "I'll keep that in mind."

"Speaking of murder, which we really weren't, but I'm in the middle of a new case." I plucked several of the freshest carnations from the vase.

"Really? Guess I'm not surprised. Murder does tend to follow you around. Who died this time?" Dash hopped up on a stool while I pulled together a first date arrangement.

"A young man who was a member of the bird watching society that came to town for the bird convention."

"Ah, there's a bird convention in town. That would explain the van I passed on its way up Myrtle Place just now. The side of the van mentioned some West Coast Bird Watching Society. I think they were heading up to the Hawksworth place to look for birds."

I nearly dropped the cluster of carnations. "You saw them just now? Heading up to Hawksworth?"

"Sure did. Do you know them?" It suddenly dawned on him. "Is that the group whose member was murdered? Guess they weren't too broken up about it if they went right on with their outing."

"The guy who died was not exactly loved. He had some bad personality traits, which, I can only assume, led to his untimely demise." The cellophane wrapper crinkled as I yanked a large square free from the spool. There was an urgency now for me to finish the bouquet. I needed to finish and close up the shop. I had a sudden urge to head up to the Hawksworth site. It seemed like the perfect opportunity to talk to some of the club members and find out what they were thinking about the murder. If I got lucky, I might even spot the most elusive bird of all—a cold-blooded killer.

CHAPTER 22

I'd rushed to close up the shop and went directly home to drop off Kingston and feed Nevermore. I flew right back out the door to head up to the Hawksworth house before the sun was too low for bird watchers. I decided to walk and was breathing hard by the time I reached the top of Maple Hill, but I'd been rewarded for my efforts. The society's van was still parked at the site.

Faces looked more familiar now, but the only people I knew by name were Minnie and Andrew. There was no sign of Ivy or Nora in the group. The club members stood in patches of two or three, with binoculars glued to faces as they stared off into the horizon. The Hawksworth mansion, dilapidated as it was, still hadn't lost its million dollar view. If you stood in the right place and looked the right direction, you could see the beach and the tops of the town shops. Another direction gave you a scenic view of the dense forest on the Mayfield side. The opposite direction afforded a patchwork green view of the farms on the Chesterton side.

Minnie was the first to lower her binoculars and notice me. Her cheeks rounded as she swished toward me in a long colorful skirt. She had replaced the large hoop earrings with dangling beaded strands. They shimmered in the late day sunlight glinting off the old relic of a house.

"How did you find us?" Minnie asked. "If I didn't know any better, I'd think you were following us." There was just enough accusation in her tone to make me think it wasn't a hundred percent in jest.

"It just so happens that I live right down there in the house with the tan shingle roof." I pointed toward my rooftop and produced a polite grin. "I saw the van up here and thought I'd come see how all of you are doing."

Minnie adjusted the binocular strap around her neck. "Andrew thought a few of us would like to get out and you know, clear our heads. It's been such a dreadful day. Of course, John didn't come. He's very distraught. He was close with Mason." She glanced back at the others. Andrew seemed to be looking at me with the same suspicion Minnie had just seconds before. I supposed it was rather coincidental to see me yet again on such an eventful day.

"Yes, I met John earlier. He was quite upset."

Minnie nodded. "It was sort of an odd friendship, if you ask me. Everyone likes John. He's polite and amiable. I hate to speak badly of him, but Mason didn't have any of those qualities. Mason even treated John badly occasionally. Still, they were good friends, so naturally, we all feel quite sorry for John."

I perked up. "Mason treated John badly?" I said as a question hoping to hear more.

Minnie spotted movement in a tree behind me and lifted her binoculars for a second. Lines scrunched up next to her eyes as she adjusted the eye pieces. Just as quickly, she lowered them. "Only a pigeon. Yes, Mason wasn't directly mean to John, but he would borrow his equipment and treat it shabbily. John was too nice. He allowed Mason to walk all over him and take advantage of his kindness. You know, typical one-sided, toxic friendship."

Andrew was apparently curious about our conversation. He peeled away from the others and crossed the lot to us. "Interesting seeing you here," he said. There was that suspicious tone again.

"It turns out she lives right down there." Minnie pointed to my rooftop. "She spotted the van and came up to check on us. Isn't that nice?"

Andrew nodded. "Kind of you. All of us are in shock still, but a few of us thought it would be therapeutic to go out birding. Now that I'm seeing the view up here, I think it'll be a beautiful place to watch the sunset."

"Yes, it's quite impressive up here," I concurred.

"Have they arrested Nora?" he asked casually, but it stunned me nonetheless.

"No, I don't think so. Why do you ask?"

Minnie and Andrew exchanged a knowing glance. "It's just that after what we all witnessed at the convention and the fact that Nora's knife was found at the scene, with blood," Andrew said and looked at Minnie for confirmation to continue. Minnie responded with a nearly imperceptible nod. "Then there was the incident before we sat down for sandwiches at the park."

A rush of giddiness bolted through me. Had I stumbled onto new evidence? Was my intuition about Nora entirely wrong? "The incident before the picnic—" I said, leaving it open ended and hoping desperately he would fill in the blank (all without trying to seem desperate).

Andrew took Minnie's brief nod as his permission to continue. "Nora had sat down with a few of the club members to eat her sandwich. Mason just couldn't leave well enough alone. He'd already humiliated her terribly at the slideshow. He was sitting a few tables away. He stood up and shouted to everyone that Nora had been hysterical this morning when she saw him at the coffee shop. She threatened him with all kinds of stuff, bird attacks, deadly illness. She left right after that."

Minnie, who was unusually silent, huffed. "Of course, when a woman is angry and yelling it's labeled as hysteria."

"Yes, isn't that ridiculous," I said in firm agreement. "And I witnessed the entire thing. She wasn't hysterical, and I never heard deadly illness mentioned. She was upset, but I walked her to my flower shop and she calmed right down."

Both were surprised that I'd witnessed the one-sided altercation.

"So you saw Nora attack him?" Andrew was apparently stuck on the whole hysteria thing.

"No attack just a few good verbal assaults tossed his way. And Mason smirked and smiled and teased her," I said. "It would have been a good opportunity for him to apologize for destroying her in front of her peers. Even if she was wrong to put in a plagiarized photo, he could have told her he hadn't meant to be so cruel."

Minnie snickered. "Mason Fanning took pride in his cruelty. Look where that got him."

"Yes," Andrew said with a solemn head shake. "He pushed poor Nora right over the edge, and now she'll spend a lifetime in prison."

"We don't know for sure she did it," Minnie said. "We should wait for the police to let us know before we start any rumors. Poor Nora has been through enough."

Andrew took the scolding mildly. "Sure, we'll let the police do their job, but I think most of us know the ending to the story."

It seemed Andrew had already convicted Nora of the crime. It was hard to blame him. What Mason did to her would have pushed anyone into a rage.

"I see the rest of you are getting along all right after the shock, so I think I'll head back down the hill to my house. Enjoy the sunset. It should be beautiful this evening."

"Thanks, we're looking forward to it, "Andrew called as I walked away.

It was a slightly disappointing trek up the hill. The only new information was that Mason hadn't ended his streak of cruelty. It was no wonder Nora left the picnic to be on her own. Or had she left the picnic to hide in the forest to wait for her victim? It seemed nothing was off the table yet.

$\mathcal{T}$hat's my favorite dress," Briggs said as he pulled out my chair and smiled appreciatively at my yellow gingham sundress.

"You said that same thing about the blue dress I wore last Saturday." I sat down, scooted my chair across the rustic red tile floor of the restaurant and smoothed my dress down on my lap.

"Then maybe it's just the model that's my favorite." Briggs had pulled on a dark green t-shirt and black jeans. I loved him in his detective suit, but casual Briggs was also a treat.

He pulled out a chair across the round table. The quaint cozy interior of Mama Jean's Italian Restaurant was dotted with tiny tables that were lit with overhead pendants that cast a warm glow over everything. The larger tables and booths for families and large groups were in a separate room, but the front room was used for couples and parties of two.

William, a tall, elderly man, who was slightly hunched from years of carrying food trays, was our usual server. "Ah, Lacey and James, good to see you," he said with the fake accent he'd created during his twenty-five years of serving pasta and bread for Mama

Jean. (William had grown up in Oklahoma.) The name Mama Jean and the copious amounts of butter slathered garlic bread being passed around the restaurant in wicker baskets made one picture the chef-owner as a short, round gray haired Italian grandmother. But in reality, Mama Jean was a tall, statuesque woman with gray streaks that only added to her sophisticated appearance. She had spent her first ten years growing up on a vineyard in Italy, then her father moved everyone to America. She returned to Europe to train as a chef and then brought her amazing culinary skills back to the states. We were the lucky recipients of her talents.

"The usual bottle of wine?" William asked.

Briggs looked to me for approval.

"Sure. I've had a long day, and it sounds relaxing." I picked up the menu, even though I was pretty sure I was going to order the mushroom ravioli.

Briggs didn't even bother to open his. He'd mentioned Mama Jean's lasagna at least three times on the drive to the restaurant.

I put my menu down as William returned with the wine. He poured us each a glass. "Looks like you're ready to order."

"Mushroom ravioli." I collected the menus.

"Lasagna."

William nodded. "I'll be right back with the garlic bread and salad."

I sat up and placed my napkin on my lap. "Tell me all about the case."

"So much for relaxing over a glass of wine." Briggs unfolded his napkin.

"I wanted to fill the gap of time between now and when the basket of bread lands on the table. After that, I'll be too dizzy headed with the scent of garlic and melted butter to comprehend what you're saying." The restaurant itself had enough fragrances to push a person with my nose into a semi-conscious state. Fortunately, I'd been in Mama Jean's so often I knew what to expect and had adjusted my nose accordingly. Plus, there was such a plethora of aromas, onions, tomatoes, garlic and oregano, that each one sort of muted the other giving my olfactory cells a fighting chance to sort them all out and put them on mute.

Briggs finished a light laugh over my dizzy headed comment. "Something tells me you know more than me," he started. "However, I do have the advantage of forensics reporting to me first. A rarity these days." He finished with a pointed look. "The knife had Mason's blood on it. As expected, the handle of the knife had been wiped clean of prints. The blade matches the chest wound. It punctured his heart and killed him fairly quickly, some time between eleven and twelve-thirty in the afternoon. He wasn't dead long before his half hidden body was discovered. Some light bruising under his arms indicated just as we expected. The killer dragged Mason from the tree where he was stabbed to the shrub in an apparent botched attempt to hide the body."

"Was there a struggle?" I took another sip of wine and glanced impatiently around for William and the bread basket.

"No, which leads me to believe the killer knew Mason, possibly stopped to talk to him before unexpectedly plunging the knife into his chest. The blade was forced in and up, which of course does terrible damage. That means the person—" he started.

I put up my hand. "Wait, let me see if I know. The person was either much shorter than Mason, hence the upward thrust." I demonstrated briefly. "Or the person knew that the upward thrust would do more damage than straight in."

Briggs smiled. "Well done."

I sat forward with a sudden revelation. "Which means Nora might have done it after all." I knew I'd spoken too loudly, catching the attention of others, and instantly shrank back and pressed a finger to my lips. "Oops," I said around my finger. "What about the binoculars? Any prints?"

Briggs shook his head. "Only Mason's. It seems they broke off while Mason was being dragged to the shrub."

Garlic streamed toward my nose, and my mouth watered in anticipation of the yummy bread. William lowered the basket onto the table. "I put in a few extra slices." He nodded at me before gliding away.

After a few silent seconds of feasting on the delicious bread, we returned to our conversation. "Nora hasn't been crossed off the list," Briggs said. "While it's hard to find many people in the bird watching group who considered Mason a friend, or for that matter, even worth knowing, I still haven't found any motive for wanting him dead. Other than the humiliation Nora endured in front of her bird watching buddies."

The door to the restaurant opened, allowing the last bits of daylight to stream in. Dash and his date flowed in with it, two highly attractive people made even more glorious by the early evening glow from outside the dimly lit restaurant.

The woman on Dash's arm looked like a Tiffany with honeyed highlights in light brown hair and round, blue eyes. Together, they were extraordinary enough to turn a few heads in the restaurant. As much as I loved seeing Dash, I crossed my fingers that the hostess would sit them far enough away that Dash wouldn't spot us at our little table in the shadows. Even though they'd put some of their differences behind them, Briggs was still never happy to see my neighbor.

That same neighbor's bright white smile gleamed in the dimly lit room as he spotted me with a buttery chunk of bread between two fingers. He waved and I lifted my bread in toast.

Briggs caught the gesture. "Who are you showing your bread to?" He glanced back over his shoulder and spun back toward me with a less amused grin. "Oh, I see."

Dash's smile had faded too. Naturally, the hostess led them right past our table. It would have been more awkward for us not to greet each other, so Dash paused. "Evening, neighbor." He gave Briggs a cursory glance. "Briggs."

"Vanhouten," Briggs muttered back with the least energy any person could use in a greeting.

Dash placed his hand behind his date's back. "Lacey, James, this is Tiffany. Lacey is my neighbor. She owns a flower shop in Port Danby."

Tiffany's eyes sparkled. "Is that where the beautiful bouquet came from? Nice to meet you."

"You too," I said. "Glad you liked the bouquet. Seems as if Dash knew exactly the flowers to pick."

"Did you get a chance to talk to the bird watchers up at the Hawksworth place?" Dash's question snapped Briggs to attention. I could feel the heat of his questioning stare on my face as I talked to Dash.

"Yes, thank you for letting me know you saw that van head up the hill," I said.

Just then, the restaurant door opened and my stomach sank. It seemed our relaxing dinner was going to come with its own splash of drama. Kate Yardley, the stylish, confident owner of the Mod Frock Boutique walked inside. She was also Dash's ex-girlfriend, although Kate hadn't really swallowed that notion fully. It didn't help that Dash occasionally still went out with Kate. Tonight, she had a new boyfriend, one of many, so many I found myself rarely bothering to remember their names. He was a tall, broad shoul-dered guy with slightly greasy hair and a face where all the features seemed just a little too close together.

Without alerting Briggs or Tiffany, I discretely managed to tap my toe against Dash's. He glanced at me. I sent a mostly invisible head tilt toward the door.

Dash looked toward the door. I was sure I heard a quiet groan. "Well, we won't interrupt your dinner. Looks like Lacey is enjoying that bread," Dash added with a chuckle before briskly moving

Tiffany along toward their table. It seemed they would be seated just three tables away. Our quiet dinner alone was feeling far less romantic.

I'd hoped a crisis had been averted when Dash took Tiffany to the table and out of Kate's view, but the woman had a sixth sense when it came to Dashwood Vanhouten. When the hostess tried to steer Kate and her date to a table near the front door, she said something and waved her hand toward the back of the room where Dash and Tiffany were sitting. Kate also made a point to stop at our table to say hello.

Kate and I were on seemingly friendly terms, only I wasn't altogether certain. Occasionally, she was cold and aloof, and other times, she spoke to me as if we'd been best buddies since grammar school. Apparently, this evening, it was the latter.

"Lacey, James," she said with gratuitous cheer. "This is Marcus." She lightly tapped Briggs on the shoulder. "I hope I can call you James when you're with my friend, Lacey." Kate had a unique and enviable sense of style. I loved everything she wore. She was like a chameleon. She could change her hair color and makeup style to suit her clothes, and it was always exactly right. This evening she had an adorable pink beret pulled over auburn hair. Her bangs were long and fringy and nearly clashed with the extravagant fake eyelashes she was sporting. Her green leather mini skirt was paired perfectly with a black and white checked tank top. And she was wearing her signature shiny white go-go boots. She pretended to look nonchalantly to the back of the restaurant, but it was easy to see right through her strategy.

"Oh my gosh, Dash, you're here too?" Her sing-song voice carried through the restaurant catching everyone's attention. She waved long, pale pink nails his way. Dash waved quickly back before hiding behind his menu. His tall physique fidgeted in the dining chair. Briggs was holding back a grin. It seemed seeing Dash squirm had added a little spark back to his evening.

Seemingly bored of her good friend, Lacey, Kate dragged her somewhat reluctant date off to greet another good friend. Dash looked as if he was ready to crawl under the table, but he forced a smile and introduced Tiffany to Kate.

William returned to our table with the food, but it was hard not to focus on the evening's entertainment.

"Poor Dash," I said quietly as I picked up my fork.

"Yeah, poor Dash," Briggs repeated, only he was wearing a grin when he said it. I told myself it was because he finally had that dreamed about plate of lasagna sitting in front of him, but I was kidding myself.

I heard Kate's forced gracious laugh finally disappear as she had to reluctantly sit at her own table. It was a few tables over from Dash's, but I was under no illusion. Dash's dinner date had just been obliterated.

Briggs enjoyed a few bites, struggling with a strand of unbreakable cheese both times. He finally took a second to breathe. "Are you going to tell me about your excursion up to Hawksworth manor? Why is it whenever I end a conversation with 'stay out of danger', you head straight toward it."

I waved a fork impaled ravioli at him. "Maybe you should stop saying it," I suggested. "Besides, there was no danger. Dash came in to buy flowers. He mentioned he saw the bird watching van heading up Myrtle Place toward the Hawksworth property. I decided it was my opportunity to talk to a few of the members to find out which direction they were leaning on the possible killer. All binoculars point to Nora," I said before he could ask. "I did learn of one other incident between Nora and Mason. I didn't get to witness it firsthand this time, but according to a few people at the lunch in Mayfield Park, Mason teased and made fun of Nora while she was eating her sandwich. She got up and left the park after that. Unless," I started.

Briggs peered up from his cheesy bite. "Unless she hid in the forest to carry out her plan to kill Mason."

"Exactly. Yet, I'm still not convinced she did it," I added.

"Me either." He plowed back into Mama Jean's towering lasagna, and I plucked up another ravioli.

"After this somewhat eventful dinner out, I could sure use an ice cream cone. Hopefully, things will be quieter at the ice cream shop," I said.

"What about the dish of spumoni that comes complimentary at the end of the meal?" Briggs asked.

"Spumoni, schumoni. I'm in the mood for butter pecan."

Briggs nodded. "I like a girl who knows what she wants. Butter pecan it is."

$\mathcal{I}$ stared at the jumbo scoop of butter pecan. "This ice cream might have been too ambitious after a plate of ravioli and three pieces of garlic bread." I took a generous nibble and used my lips to warm my front teeth after the frosty bite. "Hmm, but it is delicious, and as Lola and I have concluded, there is always room for dessert because of the well known but rarely discussed dessert stomach."

"I'm not sure I'm aware of this dessert stomach." He took a bite of the green scoop of mint chip ice cream. "Yet, I downed an entire plate of lasagna and half of your ravioli, and I still have room for this ice cream."

"See, that's because of the elusive dessert stomach. We highly evolved humans have them, so there is always room for a cookie or brownie or ice cream cone."

Briggs and I carried our cones out to the benches on the sidewalk. The sun had set, but it was a balmy night, perfect for watching stars, eating ice cream and discussing murders.

"I don't know about you, but I could sense the thick tension in the air at Mama Jean's." I turned my cone to a side that had more pecans. "I wonder how things went after we left."

Briggs wasn't hiding his grin. "Don't know but I found it entertaining to watch Vanhouten squirm. Dash never squirms, so this was a first."

"Taking just a little too much glee in someone else's misfortune but I suppose he sort of deserves it. Just when I think he's had more than enough of Kate Yardley, I see them getting a hot dog on the wharf or sitting on his front porch chatting. He keeps giving her hope."

Briggs looked over at me. "Glad to see you have at least one negative thing to say about him."

I elbowed him, harder than expected. The scoop of mint chip almost rolled off. For a long time, it seemed Dash was interested in me as more than a friend and neighbor. It had only caused a sharper division between the two men who had started as high school friends and ended as enemies. Even though there could be no doubt left that Briggs was the one for me, I'd been permanently stuck in the middle of their squabble.

"I'm sorry I brought it up," I said. "Let's switch topics to one that is far more interesting. I'm trying to construct a timeline in my mind about the murder. It seems both Mason and Nora were at the picnic when it started but then they each took off for their own birding adventures."

"Or at least Mason did." Briggs was doing catch up on melted drips with his napkin and tongue.

"Right, Nora might have disappeared for an entirely different purpose than scanning the coast for Shearwaters."

"Shear-what?" he asked.

"Shearwaters. They're a coastal bird that is normally not seen until fall," I explained as if I actually knew what I was talking about.

"If they're not around until fall, why was she looking for them?"

"Apparently, with bird watching, it's all about spotting the rare or out of season bird. That's how Nora's whole mess got started. She claimed to have taken a photo of a rare bird, only she had stolen the photo from another photographer." I, too, was chasing the drips around my hand with a napkin. It seemed we were both going to end up a sticky mess. (Maybe a balmy night wasn't always perfect for ice cream.)

"My detective sense tells me that the person who killed Mason didn't steal the phone or camera because they were special or extra valuable. Something must have been on the devices. Something that might be valuable."

I nodded. "I agree. Mason told John he had captured an image of something. Too bad he didn't give his friend more details. It could have been helpful."

"It sort of makes me wonder why he was so cryptic about it, especially to his good friend." Briggs grunted and wrapped the remainder of his cone in the mostly sticky napkin. "I give up on this. It's strange to say, but it's too warm for ice cream."

I was also losing the battle against the dripping butter pecan. I joined him in putting my cone to rest by wrapping it in the napkin.

We threw away the mushy cones and headed back inside for a few more napkins. The kid scooping ice cream behind the counter had a good chuckle as we attempted to rid ourselves of the melted ice cream.

"Glad we made somebody's night," Briggs quipped as we stepped back out into the warm night air.

"I did my informal interviews up on Maple Hill this afternoon," I said as we headed back to his car. "Did you interview anyone except Nora after I headed back to work?"

We climbed into the car. "Most of the members had each other as alibis. Everyone was socializing and enjoying the picnic during the hours when Mason was killed. Most people had the same unpleasant opinion of the victim. Apparently, Mason Fanning was always starting arguments. A few people even saw him arguing with Andrew, the club president, the night before, at the convention."

"Oh really? People do seem to generally like and respect Andrew. What was the fight about?"

"No one seemed to know for sure, but Andrew had an alibi. After the sandwiches were eaten, he went off on a bird watching hike with the treasurer—"

"Minnie," I said.

He paused and smiled over at me. "Yes. Of course you knew that. The group also included a few members who were visiting from Germany. Those interviews were brief and a little jumbled, but they all confirmed they were together on a mid-lunch expedition. They were in the same area as the murder, but no one heard or saw a thing."

"That's pretty wild to think that a grown man was stabbed and dragged across the forest and no one saw or heard anything." I sat forward to get a better look at him while he was driving. "Unless —" I said.

"Unless what?"

"Unless it was a group effort. Mason was not liked. That is one fact about this case that we've confirmed over and over again. Maybe after the drama with Nora the night before, the entire club got together and said let's get rid of Mason." I sat back, satisfied with my theory.

"It was a club. Couldn't they have just kicked him out?"

I shrugged. "That would be the easy way, of course. But my idea is far more intriguing."

"Yes, it is. However, I've found, in my years of solving many crimes," he added unnecessarily and a little annoyingly, "when there is a group of co-conspirators, one person generally caves immediately out of guilt and a sense of self-preservation. It's much easier to work a deal with the prosecutor if you come clean first and provide details to convict the others."

"All right. I suppose that makes sense, but I'm not taking it off my list."

"That's fine and I'll buy you a new ice cream on a cooler evening if your theory turns out to be right."

CHAPTER 25

*A*melia was already standing at the shop door when I arrived. She was even more prompt than my Aunt June, a woman who showed up to every social event at least thirty minutes before the actual start (a habit that annoyed my mom to no end). I sensed that this time she wanted to get to work early to talk to me without Barbara hearing.

Her sweet smile was more pursed than usual as I greeted her and turned to unlock the door. "I was thinking," Amelia said before I'd even pulled my key out of the lock. "My neighbor, her name is Molly, she's a super nice person, a little hard of hearing but really friendly." I wasn't exactly sure where she was going with the flattering description of her neighbor.

Kingston headed to his perch, and we walked to the office to put away our things. I flashed her an encouraging smile to let her know I was listening.

"Anyhow, Molly is a whiz in the garden. A real green thumb," she continued. "At least the thumb that isn't twisted from arthritis."

"Oh, I'm sorry to hear that," I said. "She sounds like a nice neighbor to have."

"She's the best." Amelia shoved her backpack purse into the cupboard we'd designated for personal belongings. "Even so, she powers right through her pain to grow the most beautiful garden in the neighborhood." We headed back to the front of the shop to start our morning routines. "Poor Molly has been really lonely and bored since her husband, Burt, died, three years ago."

"Again, I'm sorry, but I'm glad she's found joy in gardening." I pulled a treat out of the can for Kingston. (It was the first thing to do on my routine list, otherwise I wouldn't be able to do anything else.)

"I was thinking that maybe Molly would be good at arranging flowers. She really does have a magical touch with blooms." Amelia lifted her hands. "Unlike these crab claws. Maybe you could consider hiring her to help—"

"Amelia," I said with a heaping dose of sympathy. "I'm sure Molly is a wonderful gardener and a sweet woman, but that doesn't necessarily mean she can create bouquets. That takes a special skill. I know Barbara is difficult, but I'm in the height of bridal season and I need her speed and expertise. I'm hoping she'll ease up on forcing her unwanted advice on us. In the meantime, I'm reminding myself to ignore her. I hope that's not going to be too hard for you, Amelia. I don't want to lose you. You're a great assistant and the customers love you."

My last two comments helped bolster her courage. A smile appeared from ear to ear. "I love working here, and I love helping customers. I suppose I can just try harder to ignore her pushiness."

"Great. And I promise you, my usual flower arranger is much easier to get along with. Ryder is absolutely wonderful. You two will get along well."

Our timing was perfect. We'd finished our conversation and our resolve to ignore Barbara's more annoying qualities just as she walked inside. Her cheeks were full as if she was bursting with news to tell.

"My hometown of Mayfield has become quite the crime riddled city," Barbara said before hurrying off to the office to put away her things.

I glanced at Amelia to see if she had any idea what Barbara meant.

Amelia shrugged. "Don't look at me, I live in Chesterton where the biggest crime is teenagers knocking down trash cans."

Barbara's heels clacked the hallway as she brusquely returned to the front of the shop. "Should I start on the lilac centerpieces?" she asked.

"Yes, that would be great, but are you going to fill us in on why Mayfield is a crime riddled city?"

"It seems there is a serial killer on the loose." Barbara announced it almost flippantly as if she was telling us it was going to rain.

Amelia gasped. "A serial killer? Like Jack the Ripper?"

"Yes, well, I mean, I don't know if it's risen to that level yet, but there's been a second murder. A friend of mine who works for the park service texted me that they found a body on the rocks near Mayfield Park this morning." She scurried off to get the vases of lilacs.

I turned to Amelia. "A second body, that's shocking."

Amelia giggled quietly. "Yes but I was just as shocked to learn that she has a friend," she whispered.

We both finished our brief moment of amusement by the time Barbara returned with the two containers of lilacs.

Since work in the shop was in full swing, I took the opportunity to slip back to the office and text Briggs about the body.

"Is it true there's been a second body discovered near Mayfield Park? Don't keep me waiting. Your investigative partner is anxious to hear details." There was no immediate response, and something told me it would be delayed if there was another body. I headed back out to help with the centerpieces and to see if Barbara had any more details to share.

I began trimming the bottoms of the lilac stems. "So, Barbara, did this friend tell you who the deceased person was? A local, perhaps? A fisherman who uses those rocks frequently?"

"Not a local. Someone visiting for the local bird convention. At least that was what my friend was told. Since the same thing happened yesterday, I can only assume there's a serial killer in our midst." Barbara spoke with so much confidence, if I hadn't already known more about the murder than her, I might just have been convinced. But I knew better.

"I think it takes more than two deaths happening in a short span of time to verify the existence of a serial killer," I noted, but another of her frustrating traits was on full display. As much as she liked to tell everyone how to act, work and even wear their hair, she never heard a criticizing word anyone pointed her direction.

With the precision and speed that had made me keep her past the first day, she put together a stunning lilac centerpiece, all while continuing with her serial killer conclusion. (It was way past a theory in her mind.)

"I've attended several of the Mayfield City Council meetings to tell them how they could clean up the traffic on Main Street and keep vandals from destroying parks. During those public speeches, I've also given them my plan for making the town safer. They've consistently ignored me on all the important suggestions, and we now see that the town is out of control. I'm definitely going to go to the next meeting where I'm sure all the talk will be about the serial killer. I'll bring my list of safety improvements again. I might even throw in an 'I told you so' or two. After all, I told them and now people are ending up dead all over town." I let her go on with her haughty tale of how she was right and the entire Mayfield City Council was wrong as long as she continued to motor through the centerpiece order. I also allowed myself a brief moment to visualize the faces of the city council as Barbara stood up for one of her regular speeches. There were a few notes being passed and eye rolls exchanged in my momentary daydream.

I didn't know the mayor of Mayfield, but I could just imagine our own less than congenial Mayor Price's face as Barbara stood up to tell him everything he was doing wrong. Thankfully, my phone rang, seizing me from the visions before I got too caught up in them.

I pulled my phone out. It was Briggs so I walked to the office to take the call.

"Hello, so I hear there's a Jack the Ripper in Mayfield," I said as I shut the office door.

"News to me," he said.

"That's not good considering your position and all. No, seriously, my new assistant is a little dramatic. She said there was another death near Mayfield Park."

The sound of papers shuffling crinkled through the phone. "Yeah, I just got back from there. It was one of the German visitors who helped corroborate alibis yesterday."

"Uh oh, that's never good. Killing off the witness? Maybe my theory about it being a group thing was spot on, and he was the first to crack so they killed him."

Briggs paused to talk to Hilda a moment, then returned to the call. "Or maybe the guy slipped on the rocks while trying to get a photo. At least, that's what his German buddy told the interpreter. The friend, who was visibly distraught, recounted the whole accident to the interpreter, who then retold it to me. Of course, Nate is going to do a thorough exam, but this time, it seems as if the bird watcher was in the wrong place at the wrong time. It seems one of those unexpected rogue waves hit the rocks and sprayed him violently enough to cause him to slip. He hit his head on a jutting rock. The injuries and state of the body seemed to match the story."

"That's a shame about the accident, but I have to say, I'm glad to hear that Mayfield isn't the new Victorian London with Jack the Ripper roaming the streets killing off bird lovers."

"You and me both," he said.

"That brings us to the one known murder, any other information?"

"No, I was busy with this all morning."

I opened the office door, and a slew of voices skittered down the short hallway. "Oops, looks like I've got customers. Guess I have to run the flower shop."

"Even though you'd rather be out solving the murder," he said before I hung up.

"You know me too well, Detective Briggs."

"That I do, Miss Pinkerton. Talk to you later."

"Bye."

CHAPTER 26

*A*fter a long morning of serial killers, lilacs and Amelia walking a wide berth around Barbara in my small shop, Barbara took off for lunch, Amelia cleaned up the morning mess, and I sat at the computer to check emails and catch up on paperwork.

"Yay," I cheered quietly when I saw that the first email was from Ryder. I clicked it open.

"Hey Boss, Greetings from the Amazon where the stickiness never ends and the insects love to bite. Still, I'm having the time of my life. However, I received a distress call from our mutual loved one. Lola said you were having a terrible time finding a floral arranger. She said your current one was so whacky she rearranged everything in the store. I haven't given the team a definitive answer on staying another month. I could always come home if it's really bad. Let me know and be honest. I heard all about the guy who had to return to his home planet. Hope he got back safely. Interplanetary travel at this time of year can be out of this world. See what I did there? Anyhow, I'm going to be on my computer putting in data for a few days, so we can Skype if you need to talk."

I sat back with a sigh. Lola was going to hear an earful from me. She was using me to get what she wanted. Lola was my best friend, but occasionally, she could be a real stinker. As much as I needed to talk to her, I desperately needed to talk to Ryder. I would let him know everything was fine and that I had a great floral assistant. And she was great—at least where it mattered most.

I opened Skype and rang Ryder up. According to my calculations it was mid afternoon at his location in the Amazon Rainforest. It took only seconds before Ryder's wonderful face popped up on my monitor. He was clean-shaven and had a red bandana twirled into a headband around his forehead. His ivory colored, loose fitting cotton shirt was clinging to him in spots. "Hey, boss." His greeting ended with him waving a hand in front of his face to scare off a tiny flying insect. "How are things going? You look good."

Instinctually, I reached up and smoothed a few curls back off my forehead. "I'm a mess. Just got finished with ten lilac centerpieces. But nice of you to say. You look—you look—"

"Hot?" he answered. He pulled at his clingy shirt, but it immediately stuck to his skin again.

"I was going to say you look like 'going home for the holidays'. You know that feeling you get when all of a sudden you feel homesick, like you've been missing something major in your life." I had not expected to feel so nostalgic upon seeing my wonderful assistant, but all the emotions just bubbled to the top. So much for me reassuring him that everything was fine.

He lowered his face, I assumed so I wouldn't catch his reaction. Then he took a deep breath, looked up and flashed his warm, familiar smile. "I know that feeling exactly. I'm homesick too. I miss you and the shop and my buddy Kingston and of course the crazy shop owner across the street. And Elsie's blueberry muffins." He closed his eyes for a second. "I really miss those muffins. Any baked item, for that matter. We eat a lot of raw food here. Since we're on Skype, I can only assume you got my email."

I shook off the bittersweet melancholy from seeing Ryder's face and sat up straighter. "Yes, I wanted to assure you that Lola was being her usual dramatic self when she told you I was having a hard time with assistants."

He shook his head and waved off another bug. This one was more persistent, so it took a few swipes. "I knew that one about the guy leaving for his home planet was baloney. Can't believe I fell for that."

I laughed. "Actually, that one was true." I lifted my hand for the good ole scout's honor three fingered salute. "Not kidding. And he said it so calmly and casually as if he was just telling me he was going home to eat dinner."

Ryder had a good a laugh. "I wish I'd seen your face. Guess that makes me seem kind of boring."

"Are you kidding?" I asked. "You're the least boring person I know, and that's saying a lot considering my two good friends, the baker and the antique seller. Which brings me to the main reason for calling you up on this funny video call that always makes everyone look like they have the head of a horse."

Ryder laughed again, then sat forward abruptly with a cough. He patted his chest and swallowed. "Darn, that's the third insect today."

"Gosh, no wonder you went off into a delirious daydream about Elsie's blueberry muffins. Mosquitoes and gnats are hardly a good substitute for pastry. But bug eating aside, Ryder, I definitely don't want you to factor me into your decision about staying longer. I'm fine. I've got Amelia, the woman I told you about in the last email. She's great with the customers. People love her. I'm thinking I'll be keeping her on permanently. And a new floral assistant, Barbara, started on Monday."

He was about to talk, but I kept going through the delay.

"She's great with flowers, fast and efficient. Yes, she likes to move things around. She's a bit of a control freak," I said as quietly as I could while talking to a computer.

Right then, Amelia knocked lightly on the office door. She streamed right inside, holding a folded piece of paper in her hand. I hoped it wasn't a letter of resignation. She shut the door and moved closer, dropping right into a hushed rant about Barbara. She was off and running before I could let her know that I was talking to Ryder.

"Barbara nearly scared away that last customer," she said in a low mumble. "Now she's decided to rearrange all the tools in the potting area. And she told me my shoes clashed with my t-shirt."

I forced a smile and turned the monitor a few inches. "Amelia, let me introduce you to Ryder."

I hadn't meant to embarrass her, only to stop her from doling out further aggravating details about the new floral assistant.

Amelia immediately fussed with her hair and straightened her shirt. "Hello, I've heard so much about you."

"And I've heard great things about you, Amelia," Ryder said. "Thanks for being such a great help to Lacey."

Amelia was in full blush mode as she thanked him and scooted back out the door.

I spun the monitor toward me again. Ryder was looking at me with a perfectly arched brow. "Doesn't sound like your new floral assistant is making your life much easier."

"Nonsense. Sure she has some quirks, but I promise you, she's great with flowers, and that's what I need right now."

Amelia popped back inside. "Nearly forgot. This was slipped under the front door." She placed the folded paper on my desk. *Lacey* was handwritten on the folded side. Amelia scurried out and closed the door.

I focused back on my computer conversation. "Ryder, whatever happens, please don't let the flower shop get in your way. Your job is here when you return, even if it's later this summer. I'll manage just fine. Lola is another story altogether, but I'll let you two work that out."

Ryder nodded. His image froze for a second and the audio cut out. "Oops, looks like we're losing the connection. I'm glad you're managing all right. I hope we can talk soon." His image froze again and the connection was lost before I had a chance to say goodbye.

I signed off and nearly forgot about the note Amelia had handed me. I opened it up. It was nice, neat handwriting.

"Please meet me at the small children's park off Culpepper Road in one hour. I have some information that I need to tell someone. I don't want to talk to the police anymore."

I flipped the paper back and forth. There was no signature. I headed out of the office.

Amelia was giving Kingston a treat and making a big show of how much she enjoyed being friends with the crow. Barbara was too absorbed in her potting table organization to notice.

"Amelia, did you see who pushed the note under the door?"

"No, I was busy with a customer. In fact, the woman I was helping noticed it on her way out."

"Barbara, did you happen to see anyone leave the note?" I asked.

Barbara looked distraught. I'd already discovered she hated not knowing the answer to something. She tapped her chin. "I think it was a lady who was—uh, I think she was walking a poodle and wearing a straw hat."

Amelia shook her head. "No, I saw that lady with the poodle. She was just looking in the window admiring our wonderful store pet." She patted Kingston on the head.

I sighed. "Then I guess no one saw who left the note. That's all right. I'll find out soon enough."

CHAPTER 27

*A*fter receiving the anonymous note from someone claiming to have information, I assumed about the murder, I was excited, slightly nervous and entirely too distracted to focus on work. Barbara and Amelia didn't seem to notice that I was utterly useless for the next half hour. They went right on doing their jobs and doing them well. If Barbara was left on her own, to arrange flowers, she was generally focused, productive and too busy to criticize or tell someone how to wear their hair. That helped create a serene, almost congenial atmosphere in the shop, which was exactly what I needed. I also needed the courage to ask the women (namely Amelia) to watch the store while I went off on an important errand. Naturally, I hadn't told either of my assistants about the content of the mysterious note, however I had decided it was probably a smart idea to tell someone where I was going. Briggs would give me a hard 'no way' if I told him what I was up to. He'd head to the park to meet the person, but the letter writer had said they were tired of talking to the police. I was sure if Briggs showed up with me, the informant would flee and the opportunity would be missed. That left one of two people to tell, just so someone knew where I was in case the worst happened and the informant had more nefarious motives for writing the note. I needed to have a chat with Lola anyhow, so the decision was easy. Besides, Lola was less likely to try and talk me out of it.

"Girls," I said cheerily. "Good job this morning. We're a great team. (A pep talk was always a good way to start.) I need to go out on an errand. It shouldn't take more than an hour." I looked at Amelia. Her reaction was about what I expected, guarded and far less enthusiastic about the notion than Barbara.

Barbara pushed a long stem rose into a rosebud vase. "No problem, we'll hold down the fort."

"Yes, we will," Amelia said meekly. I motioned for her to follow me down the hallway to the office. I'd already learned that Barbara never considered that she was doing anything wrong, so it followed that she never suspected exchanged secret looks or private conversations had anything to do with her.

We reached the office and I shut the door. "Barbara seemed to be in a focused, less bossy mood this morning, so I thought I could slip out for a bit," I started.

"No, of course, you're right. You should go. What kind of assistant would I be if I couldn't manage the shop for an hour? Go on your errand and take your time." Her words were encouraging. Her tone was not. But she was right. I hired an assistant to help run the shop, and that was what I needed from her right now.

"Remember what we talked about, Amelia. Just let her criticisms roll off of you. Eventually, she'll realize we're not paying attention, and she'll get bored of handing them out." I wasn't entirely sure about my theory. Controlling people held pretty tightly to their bossy principles, but it still didn't hurt to let her suggestions swish right by.

Amelia nodded sharply. "Yes, I will. Now go on your errand. Everything here is under control."

I hugged her. "Thanks. You're a great assistant." I grabbed my purse and keys and headed out the door and across the street to Lola's Antiques.

Lola was grunting and using *colorful* language as she struggled to move a large walnut table with massive carved legs to a corner in the store. I put down my purse and joined in her struggle. Somehow, the two of us managed to get the table 'close enough' to the spot she had carved out for it.

"I don't know why I allowed Mrs. Gregory to talk me into putting this monstrosity in the shop on consignment. These bulky relics are not popular anymore. It's just going to take up space and collect dust." With that she swiped both her hands past each other. "What brings you to my fine establishment? Are you hiding from bossy Barbara?"

"Nope, I'm going to meet an informant just like a real investigator. I'm telling you and only you in case this whole thing goes south."

Lola began setting chairs around the table, but my words finally penetrated her brain. Her face snapped up. "Wait, what? What do you mean about it going south?"

I tried to backtrack quickly. "No, not south. Just if it turns out to be nothing. Forget my babbling." I spoke fast and just as clumsily put myself right back in trouble. "I'm meeting them at the small park off Culpepper road in case I—" I came to a cliff and stopped not sure how to proceed.

"In case what?" she asked. "In case you disappear? Lacey—"

"I won't disappear." A frustrated groan escaped me. "I came to you because I thought you were the path of least resistance."

"Great, so you're going to pile this big responsibility on me." She put the last chair down hard enough that it sounded as if a leg cracked. "You know I'm not good with responsibility." She wiggled the chair and the cracking sound grew louder. "And now you've made me break the chair of this old Victorian relic that no one is going to want and that I'll have to dust and vacuum around for the next ten years."

"Sorry about the chair but that was your fault, and even though I need to be on my way, I thought I'd fill your ears with my own personal rant. I spoke to Ryder today on Skype."

That announcement sure got her attention. "You did? So, bestie, did you talk to him and tell him you could not function or run the shop without him so that he cuts short his internship?"

"No, *bestie,* because I don't want to be the reason he cuts his adventure short. That's between the two of you. My shop is running fine. Not nearly as smoothly as I hoped, but I'll make it easily through the season."

"Some friend you are," she huffed and stomped over to her counter to pull out a rag to dust the massive table and chairs.

"You took the words right out of my mouth," I said. "Using me as leverage to get Ryder to come home was a dirty trick, even by your standards."

"I thought it was rather clever." Lola began rubbing the table in hard circular motions as if buffing out an old car.

"You're really not going to sell that thing if you take off the years of charming and much sought after patina. Anyhow, I told Ryder everything was fine at the shop, so you're on your own with your scheme to get him home. I'm on my way."

"Text me when you get back," she said angrily, but it showed she cared. "You know, in case I have to break the news to James that you've disappeared."

I blew her a kiss. "Love you."

"Yeah, love you too . . . sometimes," she added as I hurried out the door.

CHAPTER 28

The park off Culpepper Road was really just a small green space with a slide, a swing set and a few rickety picnic benches under the shade of trees. I parked my car around the corner and off Culpepper Road. I saw no other cars. The area, in general, was deserted due to the fact that Culpepper and the surrounding roads were dotted with five acre farms. Low density buildings resulted in fewer people.

I pushed my phone into the pocket of my jeans. It was my only safety precaution if things didn't look right. The note was sitting on the passenger seat. I picked it up and looked at it once more hoping that something about it would pop out at me and uncover the mystery of who sent it. But the only thing that stood out to me was that the handwriting looked neat, curly and feminine. That made me feel a bit easier about the whole thing. It was silly, of course, because I'd certainly helped bring down my share of female killers, but something about the script seemed non-threatening, innocent.

I considered waiting in the car, in case I sensed trouble and needed to make a fast escape. But it wasn't exactly the behavior of a great investigator. What if the person didn't see me and decided not to stop. I would never know who wrote the letter, and I would never get to hear the information. What if they knew who the killer was? What if they'd witnessed the murder and they were too afraid to tell anyone? They'd chosen me as their confidant. I'd be letting the person down. I'd be letting myself down. I hadn't driven to the park to hide in my car.

I pushed open the door and glanced around. Two crows sat on the edge of a squat farm fence. One held something hard, a nut of some kind, in its beak and the other looked longingly at the treat. It, apparently, hoped its friend would either drop the nut or share it. My own crow would never have made it out in the wild. He grew impatient if his hard boiled eggs weren't delivered fast enough to his bowl.

I scanned the area hoping there would be at least someone out picking bugs off a crop of lettuce or planting tomato seedlings. But it was late morning, and the farmers had already finished their morning chores and gone inside to cool off from the summer sun. The same hot sun had made the metal slide and swings unusable. It would be a good six hours before the playground equipment cooled down enough for use. I was utterly alone.

I took a deep breath and walked around the corner to the mini park. A few pigeons scrounged in the grassy area looking for tidbits to eat, but they were the only sign of life. It was entirely possible the person got cold feet. Maybe they decided to go to the police after all.

I patted my pocket to make sure my phone was still there as if it might have crawled out at some point during my short walk to the park. I sat on the picnic bench and realized after sitting for a few minutes in the deserted park that the hairs on the back of my neck were standing at attention. I spun around and a pair of eyes peered past the gnarled, rough trunk of the shade tree. I recognized Nora instantly. She stepped shyly out from her hiding place and glanced around nervously like a rabbit coming out of its hole.

"I came alone if that's what you're worried about," I said.

Her stiff face relaxed into a weak smile. She came farther out from the shadows. A book was tucked under her arm. She joined me at the bench.

"I figured I could trust you. That's why I left you the note." She placed the book on her lap. Her hands smoothed over it. A panoramic photo of cotton candy pink flamingos was spread across the glossy cover. The title read *Birds of the World* in lime green lettering.

"You mentioned you had some information. I assume this is about the murder."

Just the word caused her to sneak a peek around the park. "Yes, but I'm not sure if it's important. I just thought someone should know. I thought if I went to the police it would get me in trouble with the club. They'd find out and then I'd be kicked out for being a traitor or snitch. I'm already not in good standing with the club after my slideshow. I don't need to give them any other reason to kick me off the roster."

"Obviously, the West Coast Bird Watching Society is very important to you," I said.

"Bird watching is my life." Voices rolled up the road. Two teens on bicycles were pedaling along Culpepper Road. It seemed they might stop at the park, but they kept on riding.

"Does the book you're holding have something to do with this?" I asked.

She looked down at it and once again smoothed her hand over it. That was when I noticed a feather bookmark was sticking out from the center of the pages.

"Yes, one picture in particular." Nora lifted the book and opened to the page marked with a feather. I didn't need to be too knowledgeable about birds to know I was looking at a California condor. The baldheaded bird was sitting high on its cliffside nest gently feeding its chick. It was quite the close up. It was hard to comprehend how the photographer even managed to get the impossible shot. It was not surprising to see a gold seal on the page declaring it the 2016 World Bird Society's Photo of the Year.

"That is quite the shot. How on earth did they get it?"

Nora looked up at me. "She had to rock climb up an adjacent cliff with a camera and telephoto lens. She sat up there for seven hours waiting for the mother to return from hunting."

"She? So the photographer was a woman? Good for her." Just as I said it, I remembered something about a photo that Ivy took that Mason stole. My eyes dropped to the tiny print beneath the photo. "Photographer credit to Mason Fanning," I read aloud.

"Yes, only Ivy took this picture. She used what we all consider an old-fashioned camera, the kind that requires film and developing. She was so thrilled about it. The entire society and our east coast counterparts were camping in the Sierra Nevada Mountains at the time. Ivy came back to camp exhausted and just about delirious with joy. She told us she had an award winning photo on her film. She didn't go into detail because she wanted to surprise us. We all went home from the trip. Ivy discovered someone had stolen the film from her camera. She was devastated, but there were over a hundred people on that trip. It was too hard to find the thief. A good year passed when suddenly news reverberated through the group that Mason Fanning had won the prestigious Photo of the Year award. He refused to give out any details and told us we'd have to wait for the book to come out." She tapped the book. "Every year bird watchers from around the world submit photos for the annual printing." Nora took a moment to make sure we were still alone. "You seem like a very smart woman, so I'm sure you've already put together the pieces. Naturally, Ivy put up a fuss and protested, insisting that she had taken the shot, but she had no proof. Mason had the film and the negative. He had stolen it, of course but Ivy couldn't prove it."

"I don't like to speak badly of the dead, but he was not a nice man. He made such a stink about your slideshow when all along he knew he'd stolen Ivy's award winning photo."

"He got all the credit, prestige and the five thousand dollar prize money." Nora closed the book. "You can imagine how angry and distraught Ivy was. She even quit the society for a few years. She just rejoined last year."

The entire story was so shocking, I started putting together why Nora had brought it to my attention.

"Do you think Ivy killed Mason?" I asked point blank.

My question made her obviously uneasy. She shrank back into her shoulders and made herself smaller. "I don't know for sure. It's just that—" She looked anxiously around.

It had just occurred to me after my initial fear that I'd been walking into some kind of trap that my secret informant might be in some danger of her own, thus putting us both in peril. Ridiculously, the first thought racing through my mind was 'boy, Briggs is going to be so mad if I get myself killed on this case'.

I put my hand gently on hers. "Are you worried someone followed you?"

She shook her head. "No, I don't think so," she said, shrinking down even more. Then she took a deep breath and returned halfway to her normal posture. "No, I'm sure not. It's just that I've never done anything like this before. I'm not a tattle tale." A smirk turned up her lips. "That was always Mason's job in the club. He loved to get people in trouble. But I'm off topic. Let me just leave you with this, then I'm going back to my hotel room to shelter until the detective tells us we're free to go. It's been an awful convention. We lost another member. Poor Peter, he slipped on rocks this morning."

"Yes, I heard about that." Nora was so anxious she had a hard time staying focused. I directed her back. "You wanted to say something else?"

"Yes, I'm sorry. I just can't keep my head straight. I don't know if Ivy had anything to do with the murder, but I've been wracking my brain, trying to figure out how I lost my knife. My memory is hazy because I've been in such a horrid state of mind after what Mason did to me. But I remember seeing the knife on my backpack when I sat down to eat my sandwich at the picnic. There were a lot of us at one table. Ivy was sitting a few places down from me. We'd put our packs in a pile behind the table so they wouldn't take up space. After my first bite, I glanced up and spotted what I was certain was an Anna's Hummingbird hovering over some flowering shrubs in the park." Nora smiled faintly, drifting momentarily away from the grave situation surrounding her. "Hummingbirds are a particular favorite of mine. I keep a journal describing every hummingbird observation and sighting. I find them fascinating."

"I agree. They are wonderful." I gazed expectantly, waiting for the rest.

She shook herself out of her hummingbird thoughts. "Right. I got up to follow the bird. It flitted along an entire hedgerow searching for the last blooms of early summer. It hovered in the area for a good ten minutes. When I returned to the table, some of the people had finished their sandwiches. They were milling about, making plans for the afternoon's excursions. Ivy was up and about. I sat down to finish my sandwich. That was when Mason decided he hadn't been cruel enough to me, so he taunted me about the morning at the coffee shop. I knew then I couldn't stick around with the group. He would only continue to harass me, and frankly, I couldn't stomach seeing his face or hearing his voice anymore. I got up from the table, grabbed my backpack from the pile and stormed back to my car. I was so heated and angry, I never noticed that the knife was gone."

"So someone at the picnic took the knife," I said.

"I can only assume since it was there when I put the backpack down. It has a pearl white handle, so it's easy to spot on my dark gray backpack."

"Yes, I've seen it," I added, without thinking.

Nora sat up straighter. "You have? See, I knew you were the person to talk to. Minnie told me you seemed to be close with the detective investigating the murder. She thought maybe you two were a couple."

"Minnie is very observant. Yes, I assume I'm free to tell him about the entire photo scandal?"

"Yes, just as long as I'm not named outright as the source of the information. I don't want to be kicked out of the club."

"No problem. I'll tell him the source but let him know you want to stay anonymous." I needed to get back to the flower shop to avert disaster. "Thank you for letting me know about this. Can I take a quick picture of the book so I can tell James—Detective Briggs about it?"

"You can borrow it." She pressed it into my hands. "The feather is holding the place."

We both stood from the bench.

"I hope they catch who did this soon. I hate to think that someone in the society is a murderer," Nora said.

"I'm sure that has to be very unsettling. Take care and keep in touch."

I walked quickly to my car. As desperately as I wanted to get back to the shop and check in on my assistants, I had to make at least one pit stop—the Port Danby Police Station.

CHAPTER 29

I was in luck. Briggs had just gotten back to the station, Hilda kindly informed me before buzzing me through. I'd been rehearsing what to say, to make sure the part of the story where I snuck off to meet someone who left me a mysterious anonymous note would not be his central focus.

I knocked lightly and poked my head inside.

"Hey, didn't expect to see you." Briggs hopped up from his chair. "But it's a nice surprise." He kissed me, then leaned back to scrutinize my face. "Why do you look like the kid who has something big to confess to his parents?"

"Darn and I practiced my poker face all the way here from Culpepper Road."

He circled around and sat at his desk. I was somewhat relieved, thinking it would be easier to spill everything with him sitting behind his desk. There was really no logical reasoning behind my theory, but it gave me some courage.

"I'm going to cut to the important stuff." I placed the book I'd been holding on his desk.

Briggs stared down at it. "Do you want me to start a new hobby?"

"Nope, but if you open the book to the page marked with the feather, you'll see an amazing picture of a condor feeding its chick. It won an award."

He sat forward and opened the book. It took him only seconds to spot the name. "Mason Fanning won this award," he said.

"Yes, he did, along with the five thousand dollar prize and the great prestige and admiration that came with capturing such a difficult yet important photo. Only here's the catch and it's big. Mason didn't take the picture. One of the club members, Ivy Eagleton, snapped it. And it was quite an ordeal and harrowing too. She had to climb a steep cliff and hang there for seven hours to get the shot. She was at a large gathering of bird watchers when it happened. She bragged that she'd taken an amazing photo, then the roll of film was stolen. It was quite obvious, once the picture was published, that Mason Fanning was the thief. Poor Ivy had no way to prove it was hers."

Briggs sat back and rubbed his jaw. "That's a strong motive." He pulled out his notebook and flipped it open. "I spoke to Ivy. She mentioned she was a professional photographer. We mostly discussed what she witnessed at Nora's slideshow and at the picnic."

"Speaking of the picnic, Nora told me she had the knife when she sat down to eat her sandwich. It was in the sheath on her backpack. Then she put the pack down with other backpacks while the club ate lunch. In the midst of her meal, she spotted a hummingbird and followed it, taking her away from the tables. She left the remainder of the picnic abruptly when Mason started harassing her. She said she left in such a huff, she didn't notice the knife was missing."

Briggs wrote a few details down in his notebook, then his brown eyes lifted with a questioning look. "It seems you've been out interviewing suspects." His tone was noncommittal, leaving me unsure whether he was upset or pleased or indifferent.

"I was?" I somehow managed to make the two words sound like a question, a result of not quite knowing how he was going to react.

He tapped his pen on the notepad. "Should I ask how you came to get all these details out of Nora? Who, I might add, is still a person of interest."

"You should not. Let's just say I have secret channels into the bird watching world." I hoped my light response would jostle him into a smile and a 'good work, partner' but no luck. He had the advantage of knowing I was a terrible liar.

"Lacey," he started.

I lifted my hands. "No time to chat about this. I've left poor Amelia alone with Barbara. She's going to need to start seeing a therapist if I stay away from the shop much longer."

His sigh fluttered some of the papers on his desk. "Fine. Probably best I'm in the dark on this one." He rose from his chair to walk me to the door but stopped short of opening it. He took my hand to turn me toward him. "Please don't take any more chances."

"I promise," I said. "And it really wasn't a chance. I had support personnel in place."

"If you're talking about Lola or Elsie, then that doesn't make me feel better."

I turned an invisible key in front of my lips. "Then I'll say no more about it. Are you going to talk to Ivy again?"

"I'd say, with this new information it might be a good idea. She obviously had motive. However, that book is from 2016. She's had a few years to carry out the revenge plan. That doesn't make too much sense."

"Unless it's something she's been thinking about for a long time, and the opportunity just happened to present itself. Or maybe, his terrible cruelty the night before reminded Ivy of just what a bad guy Mason was. Since his camera was missing—"

Briggs nodded in agreement. "And Mason had been bragging that he'd taken an important picture. Maybe Ivy thought it would be a good way to get him back. But why kill him?"

"Maybe it was the only way she could get the camera. Or maybe the notion that he captured some award winning photo just reopened the old wound. Maybe it just made the whole thing fresh in her mind again."

"All good points. I'll have to talk to her." He leaned forward and kissed me. "Get back to your shop and stay clear of potential killers . . . please."

"I'll do my best."

CHAPTER 30

*D*ash was mowing his lawn when I pulled into my driveway. It was great timing considering Elsie had sent me home with some leftover cinnamon streusel muffins, Dash's favorite. She'd apparently heard from Britney that Dash was no longer her boyfriend. The Britney and Dash relationship had been rocky and tumultuous from the start, and Elsie had been beside herself about it. Britney was an excellent baker and the first person Elsie had allowed to work in the bakery. Unfortunately, Britney became so distracted by her relationship with Dash, it grew into a huge problem. Elsie was so grateful to hear that it ended that she sent the muffins home with me to give to my neighbor. In a sense, she was rewarding him for breaking up with her niece. At least, it was all mutual, so no hearts were broken. If only that had been true about Dash's on again off again thing with Kate Yardley. I hadn't spoken to Dash since the night at Mama Jean's. I wondered how it went after Briggs and I left.

Dash saw me climbing out of the car carrying one of Elsie's signature pink boxes. He shut down the mower and pushed his sunglasses to the top of his head.

I crossed over to his lawn. "I come bearing gifts." I reached him. "Apparently, cinnamon streusel muffins were not a hot item today." His green eyes lit up. "By your reaction, like a kid who just woke to a new bicycle under the Christmas tree, I assume Elsie was right when she said they were your favorite."

He took hold of the box, and I followed him to the porch. "I guess this is my reward for Britney and I ending the relationship."

"That would be my guess." Nothing got past Dash but then Elsie wasn't exactly trying to cover up her reason for the muffin gift. She'd hardly spoken to him since Britney and Dash started dating. Dash had been avoiding the bakery too. Now that the relationship was over, Elsie was favoring him with goodies. It didn't take a murder investigator to trace her motive.

Dash put the box on the porch bench. Captain had been curled up on his porch pillow. He lifted his big head, and his nose twitched side to side.

"Those are for me, Cap'n. Keep that big, wet nose out of my muffin box."

Without voicing our plan, we both sat on the top step of his porch. It was one of those lazy summer evenings where the heat and activity from the day had settled a grayish haze over the horizon. The sweet smell of freshly cut grass filled the air.

We turned slightly to face each other. "I'm going to be a good nosy neighbor and get straight to my nosiness," I said. "How was the date? Did she enjoy the flowers? She seemed very nice, by the way."

Dash readjusted his glasses on top of his head. "Tiffany is nice. We have a lot in common, so it's easy to talk to her."

I wasn't getting any overwhelming sense of new romance or infatuation.

"I suppose it didn't help matters that when you walked into Mama Jean's to have dinner, half the town showed up," I said.

Dash's grin tilted sideways. "I noticed you and James sucked down your food as fast as possible. I wanted to do the same, but it turned out Tiffany is a nibbler. She took fifteen minutes just to eat a piece of garlic bread and that was leaving behind most of the crust."

I blinked at him in disbelief. "She didn't eat the crust?"

"No crust. Best part and she nibbled right up to it. That was where it ended."

I shook my head. "Well, she's very pretty and like I said, she seems nice, so maybe this one tiny character flaw can be overlooked."

We both had a good laugh, then Dash grew quiet and favored me with his brilliant green gaze.

"See, this, what I have with you, I can't seem to find that with any of the women I date. I want to laugh and have fun and not take life or myself too seriously."

"Give Tiffany a chance. She probably just needs time to warm up. She's probably just trying to figure out your character. It's hard to see past all this green eyed dazzle." I waved my hand in a circle in front of him.

"Yeah, I can see your point. I sometimes have to avoid mirrors." We laughed again. We'd gotten along well from the start. Dash had always been so easy to talk to, but something told me my theory about the dazzle wasn't just teasing fun. His extreme good looks were probably more intimidating than he realized. Not everyone could see right through the startlingly handsome veneer to the real, easy to talk to man beneath.

"James and I left, as you noted, pretty fast. How did things go for the rest of the dinner?" I asked.

"You mean with Kate planting herself right in the middle of it all." He leaned back and rested on his hands as he stretched out his legs. "The ladies' room was in the hallway past our table. Kate must have *powdered her nose* six times, making sure to say something each time she passed the table. How is the ravioli? Oh, that wine smells good. Watch that garlic bread—it's not great for kissing." He rolled his eyes. "It was quite the show." He sat forward again with a more serious expression. "Sometimes I wonder if Kate is the one, after all. She is so—"

"Persistent?" I asked.

He chuckled. "Yes, that's the word. I don't know. Sometimes I think the only reason I pull away from her is because she tries so hard. If she was more aloof, I'd probably find her more intriguing."

"Ah ha, like when you dated Britney. When she came on too strong, you pulled away. Then she left to Europe and suddenly you were smitten." I tapped my chin. "I'm figuring out something— you've got Lola Button syndrome. My gosh, I need to start writing a book about this."

His brow arched. "Lola Button syndrome. Does that mean I'm going to start wearing vintage rock band t-shirts and stretched out fedoras?"

"Nope, I think you can avoid those side effects, but Lola was always nutty crazy about a guy until he liked her back. Then she lost interest. It took her a long time to realize Ryder was the one because he showed far too much interest in the beginning. Once he backed off, Lola came to realize how much she liked him. Now, of course, the obsession is mutual, so she's finally happy and settled in a relationship. Well," I added with a head tilt, "not happy at the moment due to the fact that he's thousands of miles away, but you get the gist."

"I'm afraid I do and guilty as charged. Not sure why it is but I tend to pull away when someone tries to get too close."

Briggs' car pulled around the corner and into my driveway.

"I'll save that for our next therapy session." I stood up and brushed off my bottom. "And I'll just charge the nickel like Lucy did with Charlie Brown."

Dash stood too. "Great, so I'm poor, miserable Charlie Brown."

"Oh, come on, you know you're Schroeder, the piano playing dreamboat with the thick golden hair." I headed down the steps.

"If I were, then Lucy would be pining for me instead of the detective."

I glanced back over my shoulder to flash him a smile. "Enjoy the muffins." I headed back across the lawn to my house.

Briggs was just climbing out of his car. Hopefully, he had news about the case. He didn't look altogether pleased that I'd just come from a chitchat with my neighbor, but that was his albatross to deal with not mine.

CHAPTER 31

I sliced a lemon for some iced tea and handed Briggs a glass. "I'm dying to know what Ivy said." I sat next to him on the couch.

"Ivy was pretty upset that she was being questioned. She confirmed the entire story about the stolen condor picture, and she admitted that she was filled with rage about it. She also said she'd gone to therapy to help manage her reaction. It turned out after the rage dissipated, a bout of depression was left behind. Ivy insists she'd come to terms with the whole thing. For about a year afterward, she searched for a lawyer to help sue Mason for plagiarism, but it was too expensive and only a few lawyers thought she even had a case. After all, Mason had the photos and the negatives. She had no proof the film belonged to her."

I put my tea on the coffee table and picked up Nevermore who had been rubbing his face all over my shins. The cat settled into a deep, warm purr as he curled up on my lap. "What about the day of the murder? Does she have a viable alibi?"

"Not entirely. She said after they were done eating, she took off on the trail and eventually wandered off the cleared path to a more remote section of trees. According to her account, she spent the next hour on the branch of a large pine tree. While most bird watchers prefer to keep their feet on the ground, Ivy mentioned she likes to find more extreme vantage points like tall trees and cliffsides. She said she gets the best pictures when she pushes herself to be more daring."

"I have to say, that story matches exactly what she told me when I arrived at the picnic with Elsie's brownies. Ivy was the first person to greet me, and I mentioned the heavy smell of pine. She didn't hesitate or plan a response. She told me she'd been sitting in a giant pine tree waiting for a good shot."

Briggs put down his glass and reached over to rub the back of Nevermore's ears. It fired up the purr motor again. "Aside from seeming agitated that she was being questioned, there was nothing in the interview that raised any red flags for me. Everything she said seemed plausible and genuine."

"I thought it might be a far-fetched notion too," I admitted. "I spoke to Ivy several times. She never struck me as a killer. It's just that Nora made a special point of telling me about the stolen photo."

In typical cat fashion, Nevermore grew tired of the attention. He jumped off my lap and sauntered away, whipping his tail to and fro not as a form of thank you but as a form of I'm done with you humans for the time being.

"Maybe Nora was trying to lead us onto a different path. She is still connected to the crime because of the murder weapon. Not to mention strong motive." Briggs reached for his tea. "Wish we had something to go with this tea. You don't happen to have any cookies in the cupboard, do you?"

I looked over at him. "It's almost as if you don't know me at all." I hopped up. "Are you in the mood for something that is stuffed with sugary, greasy cream or something dipped in chocolate and coconut?"

"Hmm, bring both. I can't decide."

I carried the two cookie packages to the coffee table and set them down. "I had one of Elsie's oatmeal raisin cookies on my way out the door this afternoon, so I think I'll opt for an orange." I headed back to the kitchen and pulled a chilled navel orange out of the refrigerator.

"Doesn't oatmeal raisin count as healthy? Seems like they shouldn't even be called cookies." Briggs had pressed together one of each kind of cookie. He peered up at me from the couch. "It's called a compromise." He took a bite of the towering treat. It snapped and crumpled into a cascade of crumbs and coconut.

"Gee, who could have seen that coming?" I laughed as I plopped down next to him. I jammed my fingernail into the thick orange peel and a burst of sunshiny citrus fragrance filled the air. I took a deep whiff. "Nothing like the smell of an orange." I proceeded to peel the fruit. "I sure wish there had been some telling scents on Mason, but pine was the only thing I detected." I pushed the sweet slice into my mouth and pursed my lips to avoid spraying juice on the couch.

The aroma of orange brought me back to the bird convention. Minnie had been eating a fragrant orange as Elsie and I arrived with the shortbread cookies. Then something very farfetched and probably way off base came to me.

I twisted on the couch to face Briggs. "James, what if it wasn't a rare bird photo on Mason's camera. What if he'd managed to catch a picture of something else, something that might harm another person's reputation?"

"Like a blackmail photo?" he asked. He collected the crumbs off the front of his t-shirt. "Interesting. Only that brings me to the second piece of information I brought with me tonight."

I sat up straight. "You found the camera."

"Yep. The camera was shoved into the cavity of an old tree trunk. The phone was there too, but it had been smashed into a bunch of pieces. The camera was intact but the entire memory had been erased. Not one photo left behind."

I sat back into the cushions. "Darn. That doesn't make this easy then, does it?"

"I'm starting to see some of those cute sparkling Lacey light bulbs going on over your head. What are you thinking? Is there someone in particular who you think might have been caught doing something compromising?"

The few flickers of notions ping ponging through my brain were so flimsy, they weren't even worth mentioning. "No one in particular," I said. "But don't you worry, I'll get to the bottom of this if it's the last thing I do."

"That's what I'm afraid of," Briggs said as he reached for another cookie. "By the way, this morning I found a gray hair. That's all you, Lacey."

I wrapped my arms around his. "Or maybe you're just going prematurely gray. I'm not opposed to a distinguished gray head of hair."

CHAPTER 32

*A*fter a busy morning, Amelia was looking a bit weary, so I sent her next door to the coffee shop for a pick me up. She returned fifteen minutes later with a big grin and a frothy latte.

"See, I knew one of Les's specialty coffees would put a zip in your zipper." I leaned over to sweep flower and ribbon remnants onto the dustpan.

"Yes, the coffee is delicious, but I'm smiling because a guy, nice looking one, I might add, is talking to Kingston as if they're best friends. As I walked by, he stopped and laughed, letting me know he wasn't crazy, but that the crow seemed to be listening to him. He said, I think I've made a new friend. At first I was going to just let him think that some wild crow had taken a shine to him but then I burst his bubble. I told him it was more likely the bakery croissant he bought to go with his coffee than the riveting conversation."

Barbara clucked her tongue. "I've seen Kingston scare off more than one customer from the bakery tables. He is very brazen for a bird. Most people aren't used to crows getting so close."

Amelia and I exchanged secret eye rolls. Barbara was expert at squashing amusing situations, a real party pooper as Lola would say. On top of it, she made me worry that she was right. I didn't want Kingston scaring off customers.

"King's been out and about long enough. He'll be cranky for the rest of the day if he's out too long. I think I'll call him back to the shop." Naturally, I didn't want to reinforce Barbara's unwanted opinion, so I made up an excuse to coax him back. "I'll be right back."

I stepped into the warm sunshine and walked over to Les's shop. Kingston was standing on the table waiting politely for the customer to hand feed him a pinch of croissant.

"I'm so sorry," I said before noticing that Kingston's new friend was none other than John Jacobs, Mason's friend and fellow bird watcher. It explained John's instant comfort with a large black crow pushing himself into his morning coffee break. "Hello," I said.

Knowing full well he was doing something bad, Kingston immediately jumped down off the table.

"Hello," John said. "What a nice coincidence."

"Thank you but it wasn't such a coincidence." I pointed next door. "My shop assistant told me my bird was pestering a man for a croissant, so I came out to scold him. The bird, not the man," I said quickly.

John laughed. "He's marvelous. So he's your pet?"

"Yes, he was injured so I took him in. Then he refused to leave, decided he preferred croissants and hard boiled eggs to the fare nature had to offer. I'm actually glad he was pestering you, instead of someone not quite so comfortable around birds."

"Me too. Made for a more entertaining coffee break. In fact, any break from this week's activities is welcome." He said the last with a long, tired breath.

"I suppose it hasn't been a very successful convention. I heard about the second fatality."

John pushed the croissant away as if he'd had enough. "Yes, the stolen treasury money on the first night should have been our clue that things were only going to go downhill."

"Stolen treasury money?" I asked.

"Yes, the first night of the convention between ticket sales, new memberships and the amazing cookies from the bakery two doors down, the club had collected over three thousand dollars. It was going to be used toward our next world excursion. It's a weeklong trip to an exotic location, Borneo this year. We meet up with other bird watching groups. We all look very forward to it. Someone made off with twenty-three hundred dollars. I don't like to put the blame on anyone, but Minnie always insists on using her primitive, old-fashioned system of collecting money in a metal box. We also accept credit cards so about three hundred was collected digitally, but the box was nearly empty. Not that it matters now. I don't think any of us are in a mood for a new excursion. This unfortunate week will set us all back emotionally and enthusiastically."

Kingston, deciding he hated not being the center of attention, hopped up on my shoulder. John nearly slipped off the stool with surprise. A wide grin followed the wide eyes. "You've got him so well trained."

I reached up and rubbed Kingston's chest. "More like the other way around." My new possible theory about the stolen camera and Mason's rare and significant photo had been stirring around my head all night. Now it seemed I had an opportunity to advance my wild idea. "Mr. Jacobs," I started.

"John, please. Any person with an amazing pet crow is an instant friend in my book."

I smiled up at Kingston. "Thank you. That's nice to hear. I was wondering, that day—" I said, and by the expression on his face I knew I didn't need to clarify. "You mentioned that Mason boasted about a photo that was both rare and would have significant consequences. Do you have any idea at all what might have been on his camera?"

He cupped his fingers around the coffee cup as he stared down in thought. "I wish I knew. I assumed he happened upon a rare bird, but you never knew with Mason. He was always up to his antics." John looked up at me. "Frankly, he took far too much pleasure in causing misery to others. Bad childhood or something. There used to be this nice couple, Bonnie and Joseph, they were prominent members of the society. Joseph was an ornithologist and professor and Bonnie was an artist. She used to paint the most beautiful nature landscapes. Everyone looked up to them. Mason hated the adulation we gave them. Then, one day, he stumbled upon Joseph deep in a copse of trees." John's face reddened. "He was with one of the younger, female members of the club." His gaze dropped again. "I'm sure I don't have to add details for you to know what they were up to."

"No, I get the picture."

"Yes, so did Mason," John said wryly.

Kingston bored of my shoulder and flew off to a nearby tree. It took John's attention away for a moment, then he turned back to me.

"He showed Joseph the photo. Naturally, Joseph was beside himself. I only knew because Joseph came to me for help. He wanted me to talk some sense into Mason, but Mason was as hard headed as he was coldhearted."

"Did he try and extort money out of Joseph?" I asked. "Did he use it for blackmail purposes?"

John shook his head. "I don't think money was involved, but Joseph and Bonnie abruptly quit the society and we never heard from them again."

"So Mason used the photo to get rid of them? He didn't like having them in the club?"

"That would be my guess. Mason never told me for certain." John stood from the table and picked up his cup.

"I won't keep you anymore," I said.

"I enjoyed talking to your bird. Kingston, right?"

"Yes, after his favorite band the Kingston Trio."

John laughed. "A cool name for a cool bird. I hope Detective Briggs catches the killer soon. We're all anxious for this terrible episode to be over."

I nodded. "I think it will be very soon." I whistled and Kingston flew down from his perch and trotted in front of me back to the shop.

CHAPTER 33

My chat with John had made my head spin with the possibility that the mysterious, now erased photo had to do with blackmail or proof of someone doing something wrong or compromising. After all, why would the camera's memory be erased unless there was something on it the killer didn't want seen? A rare bird photo just wouldn't be good motive to delete pictures from a camera. It didn't make any sense. I was thoroughly convinced that Mason was trying to harm someone through blackmail. It was apparently not beyond Mason's character to torture a fellow bird watcher. I just needed to find out what he had caught on his camera that would cause someone to snap. The new theory pretty much took Nora off the list. Her shame and embarrassment had been done in person, live, in front of all her peers. There just couldn't have been anything else on Mason's camera to add to that misery.

I'd cleverly planned for Barbara to deliver flowers while I was out on my lunch break. I told Amelia it would be a long break because I was driving over to Mayfield. She had no problem with that as long as Barbara was out and about and not standing behind her pestering her about the voice she used while answering the phone or that her penmanship on the flower orders was too sloppy to read.

I reached the parking lot of the Mayfield Auditorium. There were far less cars than the first night when Elsie and I delivered the cookies. Perhaps there had been just one too many deaths to make it a successful event. With any luck, I'd find Minnie sitting in her tiny, makeshift office counting up membership fees.

Sellers called to me and tempted me with colorful bird toys and all-weather gear as I hurried down the aisle toward the utility room that was the money hub for the West Coast Bird Watching Society. John had surprised me with the information that a great deal of money had been stolen from the box the first night of the convention. Briggs had never mentioned it, so I could only assume he didn't know about it. John might not have considered it relevant to the murder case, but my intuition told me it was important.

The door to the utility room was shut. My enthusiasm and hope dropped like a stone in my gut. I badly needed to talk to Minnie. I decided to give luck one more chance. I knocked heavily on the solid door. No answer.

"Hello, can I help you?" the voice said from behind.

I spun around. "Minnie," I blurted happily. She was holding a greasy paper bowl of nachos and a drink. "I'm so glad to see you. Here let me get the door for you." It was my perfect excuse to follow her into the small office space. Even after the theft, the metal money box was sitting right out in the open on the table she was using for her desk.

Minnie appeared to be a colorful, friendly easy-going woman, just the type of person to leave a money box unattended and behind an unlocked door. Probably not the best qualities for a club treasurer but then it was also possibly not the most sought offer job. Finding out the history of her time as treasurer was the perfect way to start a conversation about club monies.

"How do you like being the club treasurer?" I asked. "It's a lot of responsibility."

Minnie sat down with a feathery groan. She lifted a chip. Orange nacho cheese dripped off the edge. She smartly picked up her napkin and put it on her lap. "Normally, I enjoy the job, even though I didn't choose it. It sort of chose me. I was one of the few members with financial skills who was willing to take it on, but after this week, I'm thinking of handing this metal box over to someone else. Let someone else carry the burden for awhile." She pushed the entire chip into her mouth and grabbed her napkin to dab cheese off the corners of her mouth while she chewed.

"I suppose this week has been extra hard because of the convention and membership drive." I decided to let her tell me about the stolen money. I doubted John was supposed to mention it to outsiders. I didn't want to get him in trouble, and I wanted to see if Minnie would share the story. She seemed like the gregarious, outgoing type who had no problem telling everyone everything that was going on in her life.

My assessment of her was correct. She swallowed dramatically and grabbed some soda to wash down the food. "This week has been one horrible thing after another. It all started the first night of the convention, the night before the murder." She paused to have another chip. I smiled and waited patiently to let her know I was all ears. Although, the whole thing would have gone a bit easier without the paper basket of cheesy nachos.

She repeated the dramatic swallow and soda sip, then placed the cup down. A napkin dab followed. "That first night I'd collected a good deal of money from membership fees and those delicious cookies from the bakery. I left the box here and went out to do some shopping before heading over to the stage for Nora's slideshow. That slideshow should have been an omen, signaling to all of us that it was going to be a terrible week."

"I felt so badly for Nora. Did something happen to the money?" I asked.

"After the horrible event, with Mason cruelly embarrassing Nora, I decided to come back to the office to calm down from the whole thing. I thought I'd get a head start on sorting the bills for a bank deposit. But most of it was gone. Stolen."

I put on a good show, hand to chest and audible gasp to appear shocked. "That's awful. Do you have any idea who might be responsible?"

"Wish I did. I suppose it's my fault. I left the box here on the table when I went to the slideshow."

I suppressed a smile thinking that the same box had been left on the same table behind the same unlocked door just ten minutes earlier.

Minnie finished another cheese laden chip. "I don't mind taking the blame, but what I really hate is the accusatory tones and looks as if I might have taken the money myself. That's why I'm going to hand off this job to someone else."

"I don't blame you at all. Well, I'll let you finish your lunch." I headed for the door pretending to leave, but I had one more question to ask. I wanted it to seem as off-handed and random as possible so as not to stir up any suspicion. My theory was still way too full of holes to take seriously. "This might seem like an odd question, Minnie, but when Elsie and I delivered the cookies you were eating an orange."

Minnie peered up at me as if horns had just sprouted from my head. The next cheesy chip stopped inches from her mouth. "Uh, yes, I suppose I was."

"I told you it was an odd question." I laughed airily. "But I have one more to ask. Did you happen to share that orange with anyone?"

Her brows inched up toward her hair line. "Share?" She gave it a few seconds of thought. "No, I ate it all by myself. Why do you ask?"

"It's nothing. Just silliness. Forget I even mentioned it. Enjoy your nachos." I slipped out before she could ask me anything else.

CHAPTER 34

My phone rang as I stepped out into the auditorium. The day's low turnout meant much less noise along with more desperate vendors. A woman tried her best to get me to check out her bird oil paintings, but I smiled and pointed to my phone to let her know I was answering a call. There was some peripheral noise coming from Briggs' end of the call, so we both had to talk louder than usual.

"Where are you?" he asked.

"I'll tell you but no lectures." Just as I finished the last word, I turned past a kiosk that was selling custom bird perches. I ran directly into Briggs. We stared at each other, phones still to ears. I burst out laughing.

"Fancy meeting you here," he said as he put away his phone.

"I was just about to say the same thing."

"I suppose you're hot on the trail of the killer," he said.

"I just might be. And yourself?"

"Same here. Because it's my job." He started walking back toward the stage area, where I'd just come from, so I turned and walked with him.

"Who are you here to see?" I had to speed up to keep up with him. "Your pace makes me think this is urgent, and the case is about to break wide open."

"Not quite but Minnie told me she would be going to lunch, and I didn't want to miss her."

"You haven't missed her. She's in the utility closet eating her lunch."

Briggs stopped so fast I proceeded a few steps before it clicked in my brain to stop as well. "You've already spoken to Minnie?" he asked. "Of course you have." Sometimes there was pride in his tone when he thought I was onto something, and other times he sounded somewhat irritated that I'd beat him to it. At the moment, it was the latter.

He pulled out his notebook and pen and kept walking.

"Oh my, this looks official. You don't think Minnie did it, do you?" I asked, again taking long steps to keep up with his stride.

"Do you?" he asked. He was still stinging that I got to Minnie before him, so it seemed we were locked in a game.

"Nope, not at all," I said.

A woman stepped in front of us with some pickle samples from the food court. I never turned down a good dill pickle, but Briggs was on a mission and didn't want to be bothered with a taste test.

I nibbled my pickle as I half-skipped to stay by his side. "You haven't told me whether or not you think Minnie did it," I reminded him.

"No, I don't think so. I just need some information." We reached the utility room door. Briggs knocked and opened the door. "Ms. Sherman, I'm glad I caught you," he said. "I have a quick question."

Minnie had finished the nachos. She was just taking a sip of her drink as we walked in. She seemed confused to see me again, which made perfect sense.

"Of course, Detective. Anything I can do to help."

I held my hands behind my back and leaned forward, ears

twitching. Briggs had my full attention, which made a faint grin tilt his mouth. "On the day of the murder, you went on a short bird watching excursion during the lunch hour."

"That's right." Minnie folded her hands, one over the other, and rested them on the table in front of her. "Andrew and I wanted to show the two German visitors some of the birds prevalent in our coastal forests." She frowned. "It's just awful what happened to Peter. He was such a nice man."

"During our last interview, you said the four of you stayed together," Briggs continued. He didn't seem to have time for side-bars or emotional comments. Something told me he had his killer, and he was just gathering loose ends to make the arrest. Now, I was more attentive than ever.

"Why yes." Blush rose in her cheeks. "I guess that wasn't entirely accurate. There was about a twenty minute interval when I showed Peter and Francis a hawk's nest I'd spotted on an earlier excursion. Andrew said he'd spotted a ruffed grouse, so he wandered off on his own with the intention of meeting back at the picnic tables."

I chirped in excitement, eliciting a fleeting scowl from the detective. It seemed I'd been on the right path too.

Briggs scribbled down some notes, then lifted his gaze. "Did Andrew make it back?"

Minnie had to think about it. "Yes, yes he did. Just after the three of us returned to the tables."

"How did he seem?" Briggs asked. Up until then, his questions had seemed innocuous to Minnie, but her face changed. The color was fading, and her mouth was drawn tight. "His usual self, I think." She nervously fidgeted with the ring on her pinky. "I'm not really sure. I didn't really think about it at the time. Do you think that Andrew—" Her words trailed off.

"Just trying to figure out exactly where everyone was that day. The first time we spoke, you assured me that you were all out on an excursion during lunch. But after Peter's accident, I was able to speak at length with Francis through an interpreter. He remembered that Andrew had gone off on his own for a section of time. I just wanted to clear that up."

"I see." You could see the wild gears spinning in Minnie's head. She knew something was up.

Briggs' next question pulled the wind from her a little more. "Francis also said that money had been stolen from the club." He glanced at the metal box. "Why didn't you mention that?"

Minnie was clearly flustered. She wriggled on her chair and fussed with her dangling earrings. "I—I didn't think it was relevant. That's a whole separate crime. I reported it to the convention security team. I certainly didn't think it had anything to do with Mason's murder." She was red faced and breathing in shorter spurts by the time she finished. "Am I in some kind of trouble? I was careless with the box. That is on me, but I had nothing at all to do with Mason's death. I didn't care much for the man, but he never bothered me. I avoided him."

Briggs nodded. "You're not in trouble. I'm glad you reported the theft to security. I didn't mean to upset you."

Minnie sniffled quietly, trying to gather herself. "For a moment there, I thought you were accusing me of something. I'm sorry." She pulled a tissue from the box on the table and wiped her nose. "I'm just extra sensitive right now because some club members seemed to be insinuating that I took the money. But what kind of treasurer would I be if I took money from the club?" She sniffled again. "We were all looking so forward to this week. It's just been a nightmare."

Briggs bowed slightly. "Again, I'm sorry for causing you any distress. Just trying to get to the bottom of this murder. We'll leave you alone now."

I flashed a sympathetic smile Minnie's direction and followed Briggs out the door.

We walked a few steps, then Briggs stopped and turned to me. "What are you thinking, Miss Pinkerton?" He was using his adorable, professional tone, but his brown eyes gazed at me very unprofessionally.

"It was Andrew," I said, succinctly, without divulging details. After all, I wasn't about to give away my whole theory without making him work for it.

"That's my thought too, only I'm not quite as confident as you. I haven't figured out a motive yet. When I asked him about the fight he had with Mason, one that a few people witnessed, he brushed it off as some heated debate about binocular brands."

"Then you're in luck because your partner has motive covered too."

The stream of visitors was growing thicker. Briggs took my hand and led me toward a quiet area that had been set aside for people to rest on a bench. Since most people were just arriving, the bench was empty.

"I assume it has to do with the missing money," Briggs said as we reached the bench.

"You assume right. If my theory is correct, I have one bit of evidence to help bring it along. Unfortunately, I don't think it's anything that will hold up in court."

Briggs looked disappointed. "Tell me anyhow. Maybe I can figure out how to use it."

"First of all, I'll tell you something more concrete, something that would possibly help the case. When Elsie and I came here to the convention the first night, I talked with Ivy Eagleton. Andrew had just ordered three dozen brownies from Elsie for the club picnic. Ivy commented that even though Andrew was club president, he was still supposed to go through an approval process for expenditures. She complained that he was always veering off the list of approved expenses. She added that it was probably why he was always having financial troubles of his own."

Briggs pulled out his notebook and wrote down a few sentences. "What was the second thing, the thing that won't hold up in court? I assume it has something to do with your nose."

"Yes, it all began with a very fragrant orange. Minnie had just finished peeling it when Elsie and I carried the cookies into that dreary little utility closet she's using as an office. The bright orange peels were piled high next to the metal cash box. The entire room was filled with citrusy aroma. For me, it was like standing in the middle of an orange tree orchard."

Briggs looked rightfully confused.

"I'm getting to the important part," I assured him. "I shook Minnie's hand. Naturally, I could smell the orange on my hand. She went to pay Elsie for the cookies, so she touched the metal box with her citrusy hands. A half hour later or so, I was introduced to Andrew. We shook hands."

Briggs sat up straight. "His hands smelled like oranges?"

"They sure did. At the time, I figured it was a coincidence or that Minnie had shared some of the orange with Andrew. I asked her but she said she never shared the orange."

"He could have eaten one on his own. It's something I'll ask when I talk to him." He wrote and spoke at the same time. "Do you think the scent on the metal box would be strong enough that if Andrew touched it to steal the money, you would be able to smell it on his hands?"

I arched a brow. "Are you questioning Samantha's super powers?" I asked.

"No, you're right. Silly me."

"Besides, oranges have such a strong smell, almost anyone would be able to smell it on their hands after just touching something with the scent."

"Good point." He sat back and flipped through his notes. His extra appealing detective's brow appeared as he considered all the possibilities.

I sat back and waited for him to look through his notes while putting together the whole theory clearly in my head. It was so organized now, I had to let Briggs hear it.

"Mason's friend, John, told me that Mason liked to get people in trouble," I started. "He once snapped photo evidence of an illicit romantic tryst, and he blackmailed the man into leaving the club because he didn't like the guy. What if Mason caught Andrew stealing from the cash box, and Andrew and he argued about it. Andrew didn't want to get in trouble or lose his standing with the club, so he killed Mason and deleted the photos on the camera to make sure no one ever found out."

Briggs smiled at me. "Maybe it's time to promote you from assistant to partner, Miss Pinkerton."

I curled my arm around his. "I'd like that but there's something we have to do first."

"Catch a killer?" he asked.

"You read my mind, Detective Briggs."

CHAPTER 35

With Andrew being the president of the West Coast Bird Watching Society, it was easy enough to track him down. He was sitting at an outside table that had been set up to catch visitors on their way into the auditorium. John was sitting with him. The two seemed to be enjoying the summer day as they sipped lemonades and ate hot dogs from the food court. A large umbrella embellished with various birds provided shade.

"Mr. Teslow," Briggs said as we reached the table. Andrew's back had been facing us, so our arrival was a surprise. His face looked cold as stone at first before he plastered on a gracious smile.

"Yes, Detective Briggs, did you need to see me *again*?" He said again with an edge of annoyance.

"Yes, as a matter of fact, I do need to talk to you."

John looked somewhat puzzled as he looked at Andrew and then Briggs. "Did they make an arrest?" he asked.

"Not yet," Briggs said.

"I don't understand," Andrew said angrily. "I just assumed you'd be taking Nora in. It couldn't be more obvious that she was the killer."

Briggs tilted his head side to side. "Actually, it's not that obvious at all. I would like to ask you a few questions if you don't mind. We can do it here or, perhaps, somewhere more private."

That request turned Andrew's suntanned face an odd shade of khaki gray.

Andrew took a showy, dramatic breath. "Fine but let me grab my hat. The sun is brutal out here." He leaned under the table and emerged with a floppy canvas hat like the kind my dad wore when fishing. It was adorned with a few pins and badges. He pulled it down over his head.

John pointed up at the hat. "Hey, Andy, looks like the red cardinal feather fell off your hat."

I pulled in a sharp breath, quiet enough that no one noticed. I held it as I sent my mind on a quick memory scavenger hunt. The day of the murder I'd picked up an unusual red feather. I pocketed it thinking it was just a fun souvenir to keep. I'd never considered it to be part of the crime scene. Where was it now?

Andrew grabbed the hat off his head and spun it around. "Must have fallen off." He was grumpy about having to talk to Briggs. He shoved the hat back on his head.

"My pocket," I said on a whisper.

Briggs glanced my direction. "Your pocket?"

I patted the shorts I was wearing. "I was wearing these same shorts on Tuesday." I reached into my pocket and felt the withered feather between my fingers. "They've been through the washer." My shoulders bounced in an apologetic shrug, only Briggs had no idea what I was apologizing for. My whole audience was more than a little confounded.

I withdrew my fingers with the washed red feather between them. It was still bright red but a much shabbier version of its former self. "I guess bird feathers don't like the wash cycle."

Andrew's face blanched as he stared at the frazzled red feather. "What is that? It's not mine," he added quickly.

"I found this the day Mason's body was discovered. It was on the forest floor near the murder scene." I smiled sheepishly at Briggs. "I thought it was just a pretty feather. It never occurred to me—"

Andrew flew over the table. The brochures and the membership cards blew up in a violent hurricane and littered the ground. Briggs took off after Andrew and caught up to him before Andrew got more than fifty yards. For a moment, I caught a glimpse of the high school football player when Briggs managed to tackle Andrew and bring him face down on the asphalt. Both men landed with a cringe-worthy grunt.

It took only seconds for a large swath of the visitors inside the auditorium to realize something far more exciting than bird toys and binoculars was happening outside. By the time a sizable crowd gathered, Briggs had cuffed Andrew (still face down on the pavement) and was reading him his rights.

It had been so much fun watching Briggs perform a totally made for television police tackle, I'd forgotten about John standing next to me until he spoke.

"So it was Andrew all along?" John's voice was dry with shock.

"I'm afraid Mason pushed his cruel schemes too far," I said.

More comprehension fell over John's face. "Andrew stole the money, and Mason had proof on his camera."

"That's pretty much the gist of it."

John shook his head. "I told Mason his evil ways were going to catch up to him someday. Seems I was right."

"You sure were. Too bad he didn't listen to his one and only friend. It might have saved his life."

Mayfield Police arrived moments later to take Andrew to jail. Briggs had a profound limp as he returned to the table. He looked to be in some significant pain.

"I was about to cheer you on from the sidelines, but it seems that might be badly timed," I said.

He gave a half grin. "Didn't hurt quite so bad when I was seventeen and wearing football gear." He circled behind the membership table and groaned as he leaned down to pick up Andrew's backpack. He rested the heavy pack on the table, unzipped it and rifled through it until he emerged victoriously with a stack of money. "Guess he didn't have time to spend much of it."

John sat down hard on the chair. "Can't believe Andrew did this. He was always such a decent guy." Minnie, Ivy and a few of the other members made their way through the onlookers toward the table. They looked as stunned as John.

"The sad thing is—" Briggs said to me as we stepped off to the side to let the club members commiserate. "The money theft would have gotten him six months tops. Now he's going away for a long time, maybe life."

I peered over at him. "Maybe there'll be a new Birdman of Alcatraz or whatever prison he finds himself in."

Briggs discretely took my hand and walked me farther away from the action.

"I'm sorry about the red feather, James. This might have been solved earlier if I hadn't stupidly put it in my pocket. It just didn't occur to me—"

He hugged me, stopping my apology midway. The gesture caused another groan. "This getting old stuff is for the birds," he said. "No apologies, you did good . . . partner."

CHAPTER 36

*L*ola spotted me climbing out of my car and sauntered across the street. "I hope you're happy, bestie. My boyfriend has decided to stay for the extra month because his boss told him he wasn't needed and that she was doing fine without him."

"I'm pretty sure I didn't use those exact words."

Lola pushed her hands into her pockets and rocked back and forth on her feet with a grin, as if she couldn't wait to tell me something that I probably wouldn't want to hear. I'd texted Amelia twice during the whole arrest event at the auditorium, but I never heard back from her. I assumed she was too busy with customers, but the smirk on Lola's face told me something had happened.

"Well, you might want to dial Ryder right back up because I think you just lost one of your assistants. Of course, I'm not privy to the details. All I know is what I saw through my shop windows as I was busy being a nosy antique seller."

I sighed loudly. "Oh no, did Barbara leave?"

"Not Barbara." She smirked. "Amelia. So I guess you'll need Ryder after all."

"Amelia? Are you sure?"

Lola cast a raised brow at me. "They're pretty easy to tell apart. I was busy cleaning my front window, all while giving therapy to your bird, who is, by the way, sitting on my counter pacing back and forth like an expectant father."

"What? Why is he there? Ugh, how could so much go wrong in such a short amount—" I checked my phone. "Oh jeez, guess catching the killer took a little longer than I thought. Poor Amelia. I'll call her and apologize."

"So you caught another psycho, did ya?" she asked.

"Not sure if he was psycho, but some people do make outrageously bad decisions." I glanced toward my shop. "I better find out what happened while I was gone. Although, I'm pretty sure I already know. I might have to fire Barbara after all."

"Probably a good idea, otherwise that crow is moving in with me for good." Lola headed back across the street. I took a deep breath so I could prepare myself for whatever awaited me in the shop. It was my fault. I shouldn't have stayed away so long.

I walked inside. Barbara was humming to herself as she swept up a pile of leaves and cut stems. "Oh, there you are. I wasn't sure if you wanted me to finish the orders that Amelia left undone."

"No, I'll do them. Where is Amelia?"

Barbara gave a non-committal shrug. "She said something about not feeling well, then she just left. Guess it's a good thing I was here to hold down the fort."

"Uh, yes, thank you." I was non-committal too. I looked pointedly at the perch. "And Kingston?" Even though I knew where he was, I was curious to see what Barbara had to say about his whereabouts.

Barbara glanced over at the perch and tried to pretend that she'd forgotten all about the fact that a crow lived in the shop during the day. "Oh, that's right. I haven't seen him. I think he went out about an hour ago."

"But I told you only I could let him out." My muscles grew a little tauter.

"Yes but he was sitting on his perch staring out the window longingly, so I let him out to have a little flight around the neighborhood. It's good for him. He's a wild bird, after all."

"No, there is not one wild bird feather on his body, and he always stares out the window. So does my cat but I assure you he is just watching the activity outside." I headed to my office but stopped and looked back at her. "Exactly when did Amelia decide she wasn't feeling well? She was fine when I left for lunch." (Especially because you were out of the shop, I wanted to add but didn't.)

Barbara held the broom with one hand and rubbed her temple with the other. "Let me think. Oh yes, she was sitting at the computer inputting order numbers, and I happened to glance at the monitor. I told her she was doing it wrong and that there was a much faster way to do it. Her face grew red. She hopped up and said she wasn't feeling well and that she had to go home. So she left." There wasn't even an ounce of comprehension in her words. Barbara was completely clueless about other people's feelings. She was great with flowers, but if I was going to have to choose between Barbara and Amelia there was no contest. Besides, it seemed Kingston might very well return to the wild if he had to stay in the shop with Barbara.

I took a deep breath. "Barbara, I'm going to give you a check for the hours you did this week, but I'm afraid this isn't going to work out for me."

She stared at me, unblinking, for a long pause then laughed. "You're so funny."

"Actually, no, I'm totally serious. Please get your things. You can come back tomorrow to pick up your check."

She let the broom drop. "Fine, this shop was beneath my skill level anyhow."

"Great, then this works out the best for both of us."

Three minutes later, with a great deal of huffing and snorting, Barbara left the shop. I texted Amelia with the news and sent a long apology by email. She texted back a smiley face emoji with the words 'see you tomorrow'.

I sat at my desk and rested back. My fingers hovered over the keyboard. I badly wanted to write to Ryder and let him know I needed him back. But I stopped myself. It would be selfish and wrong. I'd just have to get through the rest of the summer on my own. I was finished trying to fill Ryder's shoes. And I was never again going to tease Elsie about not finding a suitable assistant. It seemed I just happened to get lucky the first time when I hired Ryder, and now my luck had run out. Thinking about the word assistant prompted me to reach for my phone.

I tapped the screen.

"Hello," Briggs' mellow, deep voice flowed through the phone.

"Say it one more time," I said.

"Say what?"

I softened my tone to make it sound flirty. "You know—the thing that makes me all giddy and flushed with excitement."

He sighed into the phone. "Partner."

"Just what a girl wants to hear."

LEMON LAVENDER SHORTBREAD COOKIES

View recipe online at: LondonLovett.com/recipe-box

Lemon Lavender
SHORTBREAD COOKIES

Ingredients:

- 2 cups all-purpose flour
- 1¼ teaspoon dried lavender
- ¼ teaspoon salt
- 2 teaspoon lemon zest
- 1 tablespoon lemon juice
- 1 cup butter, softened
- ¾ cup powdered sugar

Directions:

1. Pre-heat oven to 325°. Line a baking sheet with parchment paper.

2. In a large bowl, cream together softened butter and powdered sugar.

3. Add lemon juice, lemon zest and dried lavender to the large bowl and mix.

4. Slowly stir in the flour and salt. The dough will look very moist and soft.

5. Turn the dough onto a sheet of plastic wrap and form into a disk shape. Wrap the dough in plastic and place in the refrigerator or freezer until it firms up.

6. Turn the dough disk out onto a floured surface to roll it out. You'll need to add a good amount of flour to the dough while rolling it out. Roll the dough out to ¼ inch thick and cut with a fun cookie cutter of your choice.

7. Bake at 325° for 11-14 minutes, until surface of the cookies are dry and edges are lightly browned.

8. Allow cookies to cool for a few minutes before transferring to a cooling rack.

9. ENJOY!

There will be more from Port Danby soon. In the meantime, check out my new Starfire Cozy Mystery series! Books 1-3 are now available.

Los Angeles, 1923. The land of movie stars and perpetual sunshine has a stylish new force to be reckoned with—**Poppy Starfire,** *Private Investigator.*

See all available titles: LondonLovett.com

ABOUT THE AUTHOR

London Lovett is the author of the Port Danby, Starfire and Firefly Junction Cozy Mystery series. She loves getting caught up in a good mystery and baking delicious, new treats!

Join London Lovett's Secret Sleuths!:
facebook.com/groups/londonlovettssecretsleuths/

Subscribe to London's newsletter at www.londonlovett.com to never miss an update.

London loves to hear from readers. Feel free to reach out to her on Facebook: Facebook.com/londonlovettwrites, Follow on Instagram: @londonlovettwrites, Or send a quick email to londonlovettwrites@gmail.com.

Made in the USA
Monee, IL
15 August 2020